A PONY

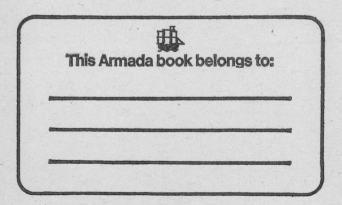

Other titles by Mary Gervaise in Armada

Ponies and Holidays
Ponies in Clover
Ponies and Mysteries
A Pony from the Farm
The Pony Clue
Pony Island
The Vanishing Pony
Puzzle of Ponies
The Secret of Pony Pass

First published in the U.K. in 1950 by
Lutterworth Press, London. This edition was first
published in 1969 by William Collins Sons & Co. Ltd.,
14 St. James's Place, London S.W.1.

© Mary Gervaise 1950

Printed in Great Britain by
Love & Malcomson Ltd.,
Brighton Road, Redhill, Surrey.

A PONY
OF YOUR OWN

M A R Y G E R V A I S E

Armada

CONTENTS

ABOUT THIS BOOK

When Georgia said that she hated horses, she meant that she was afraid of them, so it was ironical that one very brave action, in connection with a horse, should be responsible for her going to the Grange, which was not only a school but a riding-school as well.

You can imagine in what a mood she set off; and being in that mood naturally didn't help to make things easier for her. She wasn't a particularly easy person, anyway, and it certainly wasn't at all an easy term. But——!

For though she might not be easy, Georgia was one of Mary Gervaise's very nicest heroines, as Susan and Patience and Teepoo—and Penelope! —were quickly to find out. True, she went on being afraid of horses, and of the mare, Mademoiselle, in particular; but when she had helped Mademoiselle, had saved her life—and when she had a pony of her own—why, no one was surprised to hear her say: "I wouldn't have missed the first term at the Grange for anything in the world!"

CHAPTER ONE

THE HIGHWAYMAN

THROUGH the mists of sleep, Georgia Kane heard the friendly, familiar whirr of her mother's alarm clock in the adjoining room. She opened her eyes and sat up with an excited bounce, remembering that this was the long-awaited Golden Wedding Day.

"Not many people of our age," she reflected, "have great-grandparents not only alive, but in such good repair!"

It was a pleasing thought, but an instant later it vanished from her mind as a horrible suspicion dawned upon her. To her dismay she realized now that her cold, which had been no more than the tiniest tickle for the past week, had chosen this morning of all others to burst upon her with the sudden fury of a tropical storm.

"It can't be true!" she whispered, in the chilly grey twilight. "It simply *can't* happen to-day!"

A terrific sneeze soon showed her, however, that it most certainly could! She fumbled wildly under her pillow to find her handkerchief, and mopped her streaming eyes. Then she coughed. Then she sneezed again, four times, and the figure in the other bed, at the far end of the room, stirred irritably.

"Do shut up, Georgie! It isn't time to get up yet," said Geraldine.

"I'b dot—" began the sufferer, unable to speak in her normal voice—"doi'g this for fud!"

She sneezed again, violently, and Geraldine, switching on the light, surveyed her unhappy cousin with concern.

"You've got a cold," she said, with the air of one determined to make the position clear. "To-day of all days, too! What about the party?"

7

Georgie tried to smile bravely, but sneezed again instead.

"I'll be O.K., Gerry. I'll swallow quarts of quinine, and gargle, and have a bath in eucalyptus. I'll—oh, *atish*—!"

"Not again!" Gerry pleaded, clapping her hands to her ears. "Don't make such a row, or Auntie'll hear. You mustn't let her know it's such a bad one, or she'll keep you in bed!"

"I bust!" wailed the victim.

"I should think you've bust everything within miles," Gerry agreed, not unsympathetically, but with her usual detachment. "Peter says one can break a wine glass by playing a certain note on a violin, so I suppose a sneeze could—"

"I said I *must*. Tell Mother, I mean. It wouldn't be fair not to," said Georgie. "But I'll beg her to let me go just the same. I'll grovel—*at'choo! Atishooo!*"

"You get such noisy colds," complained Gerry, whose own afflictions were much more refined. "Oh, well!" She snapped out the light and lay down again.

Georgie looked at her vague outline, in the cold light of that January morning. She wondered how two girls of thirteen, and first cousins to boot, could be so utterly dissimilar. They were quite different in appearance, for one thing, though that counted for little. Gerry was fair, with cool blue eyes, pink cheeks, smooth hair, and a naturally sedate manner. Georgie was dark, with curly brown hair that tied itself in knots five minutes after it had been combed, and her hazel eyes changed colour according to her mood. Gerry was a tidy person—she never had to be told to hang up her clothes or to put things away—and she never lost her temper or did wild, impulsive deeds. "Try to be more like Gerry, dear!" That was what Georgie's elders had been saying to her for years: "*she* doesn't come in to tea with ink on her fingers, or read in the bath, or tear herself to pieces on barbed wire!"

Gerry went to a boarding-school, as her parents lived abroad, and every term her report said "General Conduct —excellent." Georgie went daily to a big High School, where she was too shy and dreamy to settle down, and her reports said "Could do better," and sometimes "Does not try." Her mother always looked grave when she read these criticisms, and her father, when he was at home, would say that he wished she were more like other girls. Georgie found it impossible to tell them that she did try. No amount of trying, it seemed, would make her fit in with the forty girls in her form.

She looked at Gerry rather enviously, though without real regret. She was fond of her cousin and liked having her to stay in the holidays, but she did not want to be like her. It must be nice to have so much self-confidence, she thought, and long fair plaits that never became ruffled; but surely someone quite so perfect couldn't have much fun?

Fun . . . The word reminded her of the party, which she now felt sure that she would have to miss. She sneezed again, dismally, and the door opened.

"Someone in here," said Mrs. Kane, "seems to be sneezing!"

Of course she knew which one it was. She came straight over to her daughter's bed, and laid her hand on the hot forehead.

"My poor Georgie, what dreadfully bad luck! I'll fill your hot-water-bottle again, and give you some of Daddy's nice big hankies."

"Oh, Mother!" Georgie gave a gulp. "If I gargle like mad, and take everything there is in the medicine-cupboard—don't you think I can go to the party?"

Mrs. Kane shook her head. She was tall and slender and pretty, with dark curly hair like Georgie's—only hers was under control.

"There's no magic to cure a cold as quickly as all that, darling. I was afraid of this when you told me you had that tickle. It's a great disappointment," she said, "but we must bear it."

"I hate bearing things!" Georgie burst out. "Oh, Mother, if I wrap myself in blankets like an Indian squaw—"

"No, Georgie. It isn't only yourself, you know. Imagine

9

how you'd feel if you gave your cold to the Great-Grandies, or to any of the others. One can take a harp to a party—you remember the song—but it isn't right to take germs."

"I'd forgotten them. All right, Mother, I'll stay here—but it doesn't mean that you or one of the boys will have to stay with me, does it? I'll be perfectly all right alone," Georgie said earnestly.

"Germs!" said Gerry at the same moment, getting out of bed. "I'd forgotten them, too. I think I'd better gargle." And she hastened away, prudent as usual.

"I expect Mrs. Duncan will stay and sleep here to-night. I'll ask her presently. You know you can't be left alone, Georgie, in this house which is nearly a mile from the village. Don't cry, my dear," said Mrs. Kane. "If Mrs. Duncan can't manage it, I'll stay, and we'll have a party of our own."

Georgie achieved a faint grin, very glad that Gerry was not in the room. Gerry, of course, never cried. She had read *Black Beauty* last holidays, without a single tear.

"Oh, Mother, I wish something nice would happen!"

"Nice things are happening all the time. Daddy'll be back from Africa in the spring, and Peter's so much better that he'll be able to go to school again in the summer. That's a pleasant thought for you, Georgie," Mrs. Kane said, as she turned towards the door. "It's largely through you that he's got on so well. Now lie still and keep warm till I bring your breakfast."

She hurried away, leaving Georgie greatly cheered. Peter, her eldest brother, was nearly seventeen. Two years ago a bad accident while ski-ing had given him slight paralysis as well as damaging his sight. He had been at home ever since, and Georgie had read to him and entertained him by the hour. This was no hardship to her, for she had always liked being with him. Georgie at eleven had no interest in the books he liked, but she read aloud to him doggedly, mispronouncing many of the words at first, but gradually coming to know them. Without Georgie, he would have brooded on his helplessness, and lost touch with the world.

The other boys in the family, twins just a year older

than Georgie, had never had much in common with Peter, and would be no use to him now. Ralph and Tony—usually known as Rough and Tough—were a cheerful, clamorous pair who lived for football and boxing, and believed that there were far too many books in the world. They admired their elder brother, who had been a fine sportsman before his accident, and they were very fond of their only sister; but they had long ago dubbed Peter "The Professor" because he read so much, and dismissed Georgie's flights of fancy as "more of that tripe". But Georgie spent most of her free time with him, and a real friendship had sprung up now, spanning the four years that divided them. He had more than repaid her efforts, for quite unconsciously he had taught her a great deal. She might not be able to work out a theorem or grasp the mysterious behaviour of x and y, but she had a fund of unusual knowledge stored away under that thatch of dark hair.

And now he was almost well again. His sight had returned, and soon he could stop wearing those thick glasses, and walk without a limp. She smiled to herself at the thought . . .

Gerry came back, tumbler in hand, and announced that she was going to dress.

"Did you gargle? I didn't hear you," said Georgie.

Gerry looked scandalized. "I know *you* can gargle from six different operas, but it's frightfully bad form. . . . Auntie's getting your breakfast, and Mrs. Duncan's come. I heard her saying that she'd spend the night here, so everything's all right."

Georgie, sneezing again, could not agree with this last statement, but she was glad that the pleasant, red-cheeked countrywoman who came every day from Dockleford village to help with the housework would be able to stay with her. Now the rest of the family could celebrate the Golden Wedding, and not disappoint the Great-Grandies after all.

When Gerry was buttoning up her best frock, with the crisp white organdie collar and cuffs which Georgie would have ruined in an hour, Peter came into the girls' room with a new anthology of poetry.

11

"To keep you going till to-morrow," he said to his woebegone sister. "It's very hard luck, I must say."

"Oh, well, it might have been worse," she responded, cheering up at once at the sight of his friendly grin. "I'm so thankful all the rest of you can go. Give my love to the old pets, won't you? And feed the ponies for me. There's a bag of apples over in that corner by the cupboard. I've been hoarding them for a week."

"So that's what's been smelling so awful—just by my bed, too! Georgie, you are the absolute limit," grumbled Gerry, but she found the big paper bag and gave it to Peter.

"You know you like the ponies, too," said Georgie.

"Yes, of course I do, but I'm not idiotic about animals as you are. Hallo, here are the Lads now, *and* the rest of the menagerie!" And Gerry, who wasn't as cross as she sounded, laughed as Rough and Tough marched into the room.

"*What* did you call us?" Rough inquired in a menacing tone, holding up the two spaniel puppies he was carrying. The word "Lad" never failed to infuriate the twins, because their Uncle Archie, the family bugbear, always addressed them in this way.

"Oh, Rough, be careful—take them away! Look what you've done!" cried Gerry, disentangling an eager black paw from her hair.

"I didn't do it—Velvet did! Now you've frightened him, shouting like that," Rough said, and carried the puppies over to his sister's bed. "Catch, George! An armful of dog-flesh for you! Look after them for us till to-morrow."

Tough now came forward, bearing Georgie's own particular pet—King Toby, a beautiful golden cat with a great bushy tail. He was immensely dignified, and his affections were few. He wriggled out of Tough's arms and purred to Georgie before seating himself on her eiderdown and proceeding to wash his face.

"I'll take the greatest care of the pups," she promised. "I suppose this is a lucky break for the animals. They'll be much happier at home than at Mrs. Duncan's place."

12

"M'm, but it's rotten for you, though," said Rough. "We've made you a jigsaw for your birthday, but you'd better have it now. Chuck it over, Tough."

"I wish I'd something to lend you, Georgie," Gerry said suddenly, "but I haven't. You don't like my kind of things. Of course you could do some of my fancy work if you'd like to—"

A derisive hoot went up from the boys. Georgie was the kind of person who never sews on a button where a safety pin will do.

"Are you all ready for breakfast?" cried Mrs. Kane, coming in at this moment with a beautifully-arranged tray for Georgie. "Well, run downstairs, all of you—the porridge has gone in, and we haven't much time. We're starting at ten, remember."

The great-grandparents lived in Cornwall, in a tiny village called Pencarne. It was a difficult, cross-country journey from Dockleford, and Mrs. Kane, who was driving the car herself, wanted to get there in good time.

She smoothed Georgie's bed, inserted a lovely hot-water-bottle, and gave her a dose of cinnamon.

"Just keep warm and try not to mope, darling. We shall all miss you terribly, and if it had been for anything on earth but the Golden Wedding, I wouldn't have left you. But you like Mrs. Duncan, and she knows just what to do. And we shall be home again to-morrow afternoon."

She went away and returned with two golden roses in a vase.

"They're from the bouquet. Ask Mrs. Duncan to put them in water. Now I must go and see if the car will start— it's very frosty to-day. Good-bye, Georgie dear."

Mrs. Kane kissed King Toby by proxy—Georgie's idea —and hurried away. There were sounds of a scuffle going on below, and then everyone called "Good-bye!" and the front door slammed. Georgie went across to the window and watched the car disappearing down the road.

"Now, Miss Georgie, back you get into that bed this instant minute!" cried Mrs. Duncan, who had come in to fetch her breakfast tray. "I'm right sorry about your cold, dearie. I know what store you sets on the old folks."

13

"Well, they are rather special," said Georgie, allowing herself to be tucked up like a cocoon. "Mother's parents died when she was a baby, you see, so she and Uncle Dick —that's Gerry's father—were brought up by their grand-parents. And now they're our *Great*-Grandies, and they're perfect darlings. We always have such fun at their house, even though Uncle Archie and Aunt Milly live there, too; and all the relations are coming to their Golden Wedding —some I've never even seen. Still, it can't be helped." She sneezed heroically.

"What perfect blooms, Miss Georgie! I declare they match King Toby himself!" exclaimed Mrs. Duncan, who shared Georgie's affection for the cat.

"The Great-Grandies said they didn't want any presents given to them, because they're so old now, they've got all they need. They're going to give things to all their guests instead. But we thought we'd take them golden roses, you see, and all the other relations are bringing things like that, to surprise them." Georgie's voice quivered. It was to have been such a wonderful party.

"Now, dearie, don't take on—though if it was my Lily, she'd be bawling her eyes out," Mrs. Duncan said cheer-fully, as she bustled about the room. "Your ma was right upset to leave you behind, and if anything goes wrong, I'm to telephone, she says. But I'm that bad at telephones, you wouldn't believe—I never seem to catch what the other person says."

"But nothing will go wrong, so you needn't worry," laughed Georgie. She settled down to read, King Toby purring majestically beside her, and the puppies playing tug-of-war with the cord of her dressing-gown.

She had just finished her lunch when the telephone rang. She thought perhaps her mother had rung up from Pen-carne to say they had arrived safely, and listened in some amusement to Mrs. Duncan's attempts to answer the call.

"Hallo? Hallo? *Hallo?*" shouted Mrs. Duncan, like an agitated parrot, giving the caller no chance to speak at all.

"Miss Georgie!" she cried at last, in despair. "Put

something over your shoulders and come down, will you? I can't get on nohow."

Georgie was already flying to the rescue, realizing that Mrs. Duncan was genuinely distressed. She picked up the receiver.

"Yes, this is Wychwood. Yes, she's here—" She listened for a few seconds, with a sinking heart, and then hung up the receiver.

"Whoever was it, Miss Georgie?"

"Dr. Warnford. He—" Georgie hesitated. This was the first time she had had to break bad news. "It was you he wanted really, Mrs. Duncan. Lily's asking for you. She's had a fall."

"Lily's asking for you. She's had a fall."

It was dreadful to see the colour fade from Mrs. Duncan's cheeks.

"My Lil? What's happened to her, then? Where is she? She's not—?"

"Oh, no! She's not dead. But she was knocked down by a lorry just in front of your house, and she's broken her leg. Dr. Warnford says she's got to stay at home, because the hospital's full. He's just going to set the leg, and wants you to go home at once."

"Yes," said Mrs. Duncan. "Yes, I'll go." She seemed dazed, and let Georgie fetch her coat and hat. "But you, dearie—what'll you do? I dunno what to do about to-night—"

"You must stay with Lily, of course. I'll be all right." Georgie ran upstairs to fetch the roses. "Give these to her, and tell her I'll bring her books and things when she feels better. I'm so very sorry about it."

Mrs. Duncan looked at her wearily.

"Can't seem to grasp it yet. . . . Dunno who I'll get to stay with you, I'm sure—"

"Don't worry about that. I'll ring up Mother, and she'll know what to do. Do go along now, Mrs. Duncan."

"You hop along back to bed, then," the poor woman said mechanically, and suddenly she seemed to realize what had happened, for she ran out of the house and down the path.

Georgie shivered, partly with the shock of hearing about Lily, and partly because she was cold, standing in this draughty passage in pyjamas and dressing-gown. She went up to her room, and dressed as quickly as she could. When she came down again, she went to the telephone. Then, her hand already on the receiver, she paused to think.

Dockleford was a small village, consisting of scattered farms and cottages. Not one of those women could be spared, she knew. Dr. Warnford was a widower, and his housekeeper had disliked the Kanes ever since Tough had broken one of the windows of the doctor's house with a home-made firework. The vicar and his wife were very old. There was literally no one whom her mother could ask to spend the night at Wychwood. The obvious result would be that her mother would come home immediately, and that would mean, not only spoiling the party, but a difficult, even dangerous, drive in the dark.

"I won't tell her," Georgie said aloud, and met the

16

dreamy stare of King Toby's agate eyes. "I said I could stay here by myself, and I can. It isn't as if I were alone. There's you, Toby, and there are the pups. I'll light the dining-room fire—I see Mrs. Duncan's laid it—and we'll have the wireless on, and you shall have your meals in there instead of in the kitchen, and we'll have a nice cosy time!"

She knew that her mother and Peter would be very angry with her on the morrow, but she was prepared to risk that. The thought of that moorland drive in the dark was too much. "And after all," she asked herself, "what can possibly happen now?"

The sudden excitement had made her forget about her cold, and in any case it seemed to have taken a turn for the better. She even began to sing, in a cracked little voice, as she lit the fire and coaxed it into a blaze, and put the kettle on for her solitary tea.

Georgie enjoyed that tea, and afterwards, in an access of virtue, she found her mother's knitting and did two rows. Then, finding that the pattern was becoming quite different, she put it away and switched on the wireless. A ghost story was being told, in a very lugubrious voice, and as the dusk outside would soon be darkness, she decided to turn it off.

Now, for the first time, she became conscious of the silence. In the ordinary way this was not a quiet house, for even in term time, when Rough and Tough were away at school, there was a good deal going on. Now, with the night pressing against the windows like a black curtain, the everyday world seemed very far away.

She had never been alone in the house before.

The furniture was old, and creaked alarmingly. Toby, her mainstay, suddenly decided that he wanted to see how things were in Mouseland, and asked to go out. The puppies fell asleep.

"Well, I can always read," said Georgie, and the sound of her own voice seemed to shock the silent room. She looked at the book Peter had lent her. She was glad she had brought it down with her. She was not in the mood

17

for poetry, but she could at least look to see if there were any old friends in this volume.

She glanced through it, becoming interested in spite of herself. Yes, there were several poems she knew, and some she had not seen before, which she knew she would like when she felt less restless. Here was one she had "done" for Literature at school last term: *The Highwayman*, by Alfred Noyes.

She began to read. Presently she looked up and out of the window. There was the moon, floating in the wild dark sky, just as in the poem. She smiled, thinking how peaceful it was to be able to enjoy just reading without having to think about spondees and dactyls!

She read on, completely absorbed now.

A highwayman comes riding—
Riding—riding—

The book fell from Georgie's hand as she heard the sharp clatter of hooves on the road.

CHAPTER TWO

GEORGIE NIGHTINGALE

FOR a second she was petrified. It was a lonely road, leading down from the moor, and it seemed impossible that a flesh-and-blood horseman could be travelling this way by night. Then, as she listened with a pounding heart, she heard those hooves slither on the hard, frosty stones. There was a crash, followed by a man's sharp cry and a horse's high scream of fear.

She sprang up then, and, seizing Peter's old coat from its peg in the hall, she dashed out of the house. The moon, that "ghostly galleon", was free from cloud, and there was enough light for her to see the horse lying across the road, making frantic efforts to get up. A man lay some distance away, horribly still.

18

A man lay some distance away, horribly still.

"Oh—!" she breathed, longing for her mother—or, indeed, for anyone to come and tell her what to do. But there was not a soul within call. Far away she could see the few lights of the village, but she was quite alone.

Her knees were trembling, but she made herself go up to the man, taking care to keep clear of the struggling horse. She knelt down, and covered the still form with Peter's coat.

"Are you badly hurt?" she whispered, touching the stranger's forehead.

To her relief, he stirred.

"My arm—"

"I'll take care of you. Don't be frightened," she said, because she was so frightened herself. "Wait here while I phone for the doctor."

But he caught her sleeve with his uninjured hand.

"Firefly—what's happened to him?" He tried to sit up, and saw the terrified horse. "Help me up—must get to him—he'll strangle himself with his own leather—"

Georgie did try to help him, but he was evidently more seriously hurt than he knew. He fell back groaning.

"Firefly—keep still, old chap. Listen, get the vet, can you? Never mind about me—"

Georgie knew then what she ought to do, if only she had the courage. She had read about situations very much like this one, and she knew that the horse was making matters worse for himself by his fruitless struggles. But she had always been afraid of big animals. She looked at those thrashing hooves, and shuddered.

"I—look here, I'll sit on his head and keep him still. You go into our house as soon as you feel able, and phone Driscoe 15. That's the vet. And the doctor's Dockleford 2. Can you hear me?"

"Yes, yes. Don't bother about me," he muttered. "Firefly—"

Georgie felt icy cold. She got as near to the horse as she could, and waited her opportunity.

"Lovely boy!" she said. "Beautiful puss-cat!"

With these words she had often addressed King Toby, when he asked for adulation.

The horse whinnied, and suddenly lay still. She moved forward and sat firmly on his head, clinging with both hands to his mane. She expected a mighty heave that would send her high into the air, but he only sighed, trembled, and seemed to relax. With one shaking hand she stroked his neck.

"Beautiful boy! *King* of pussies!"

The idiotic words seemed to please him, she thought. It was a good thing, because she could think of no others.

"Your horse is quiet now," she said, after a pause.

The man groaned and murmured something. She could not imagine how she could look after him as well, yet it was impossible for the three of them to stay like this all night.

"Now," she said, with new authority in her voice, "come over here and I'll attend to your arm. Then you must telephone."

She thought he had not heard, but after a moment he staggered to his feet and managed to get to her. He patted Firefly's side, and, at Georgie's suggestion, knelt down. His right arm was dangling, and obviously causing him great pain. She remembered first aid classes at the High School.

"I believe it's your collar-bone. Give me your tie or something, and I can at least keep your arm steady. That's it—thanks." She managed to tie the arm across his chest, though he winced and all but cried out. "Now go into the house—you can see the light—and telephone Driscoe 15, vet, and Dockleford 2, doctor."

"You won't be scared, alone with Firefly?"

"No, no. Go on!" she begged, so afraid that he might faint again.

He walked slowly through the garden gate, and she waited in an agony. Firefly grew restive and tried to get up, but was powerless as she kept his head down. She went on talking to him and patting him. An eternity seemed to pass before her new friend came back to her. He was carrying a bundle of coats.

21

"I found these in your hall," he said, and dropped them. He had managed to bring them under his good arm. "You'll get cold."

"Cover Firefly," she said, "and yourself. Is Mr. Jones coming?"

"Yes, and the doctor." He spoke quite calmly, so that it was a fresh shock to her when he crumpled up at her side. She reached as many of the coats as she could, and laid one across him and one upon the horse. Then she pulled her mother's old mackintosh across her own shoulders, and waited again. This was the worst part of the vigil. She dared not move in case Firefly should dislodge her. She was cold and sick with fright, and terribly anxious about the man, who was slowly coming round.

After what seemed several hours, but was only about twenty minutes, Mr. Jones, the vet, drove up in his car. She knew him quite well, as he had come to Wychwood several times when King Toby had cat 'flu.

"Miss Kane! I never knew you were one for horses. Good girl," he said in his bluff, kindly way. "Just stay where you are while I have a look at the poor chap." He glanced up at the man. "You go into the house, sir, and rest yourself—you can't do any good here."

He had brought two flashlights and a big torch, which he set up on the road. Then he examined Firefly, who writhed and twisted and heaved, while Georgie kept her position, clinging to his mane.

"He's torn a ligament in his off foreleg, and cut both knees. Lucky you were here, young lady—a little more struggling, and the damage would have been beyond repair." In the torchlight Mr. Jones saw the extreme pallor of Georgie's face. "Now I'm setting to work," he said briskly. "Shut your eyes, will you, and count out loud. That's going to help me, see?"

She did not see, but she understood later that he had been afraid she would faint. She counted steadily, and by the time she had reached two-hundred-and-three, Dr. Warnford arrived.

"What's all this?" he panted, jumping out of his car.

"Couldn't come before—case of pneumonia at one of the farms. Georgie, what on earth—?"

"The rider's been hurt. He's in our house," said Georgie.

Without another word the doctor took off his overcoat and wrapped it round her.

"I've nearly finished, sir. I'll send her in to you in a minute," said the veterinary surgeon, working hard.

Dr. Warnford disappeared. Georgie began to feel very sick.

"Now, Miss Kane, it's just a matter of getting him up. Ease your legs a bit, can you, and be ready to move away double quick when I say 'Go'?" There was a sound of unbuckling, and then Mr. Jones gave the word of command. Georgie, so stiff and cold that she hardly knew how she managed it, got up and drew back to the grass verge.

Mr. Jones had Firefly on his feet in a matter of seconds.

"Put him in our garage," said Georgie, with an inspiration. "The car's out to-night. There's some hay in the corner. I'll get the key."

"You're a grand lass," said Mr. Jones, and with a sudden glow she felt very proud that she had been able to help.

A few minutes later Firefly was safely housed in the garage, and she went into the dining-room, where Dr. Warnford was settling his patient on the sofa.

The stranger looked at her and grinned sleepily.

" 'Fraid I'm giving—a lot of trouble," he droned, and closed his eyes.

"I've given him something to make him sleep," said the doctor. "He'll be all right till the morning now. But I don't understand this at all. Where's Mrs. Kane?"

"Mother and the boys are at Pencarne. I'm alone." Briefly she explained how it had happened.

"My dear girl, we can't allow this. I'll ring up Mrs. Anstruther at once, and she'll come on her bicycle and spend the rest of the night with you. She'll be along in less than an hour. Now—you have a cold, you say? Into bed with you at once, and I'll dose you too! Where do you keep your hot-water-bottles? No, don't show me," said Dr. Warnford, looking very severe. "Just tell me, and then get into bed."

"All right," she said submissively, wondering whether she would get pneumonia now. She had forgotten about her cold, out there in the road, under the ghostly moon. She told him about the hot-water-bottles, and went up to her room, got into bed and fell asleep. When he brought her the hot-water-bottles and some medicine, she woke up for a few minutes, and then went off again, into deep, dreamless slumber. She did not stir when Mrs. Anstruther, tall, gaunt, and indignant, came to sit in her room, or even when King Toby, greatly annoyed by the events of the night, climbed on to her bed and made French knots on the pillow.

When morning came, however, and she opened her eyes, it was to see the doctor's housekeeper regarding her with a mixture of grimness and anxiety.

"Well, miss? Lost your voice now, I shouldn't wonder. Doctor said you were to have these tablets."

"I—I—why, I'm all right!" Georgie exclaimed—and the astounding thing was, it was true. The cold, crisp air had completely banished her cold. She took the tablets to please Mrs. Anstruther, and then informed that irate party that she was going to get up.

"That you can't, miss—not till doctor's been. Why, here he is now!" She hurried to open the door.

Ten minutes elapsed before Dr. Warnford came up to see Georgie. He examined her thoroughly, and told her that she had been lucky this time, though he would not recommend such a cure again.

"I wish that poor fellow downstairs felt as well as you do. I'll try to send in a nurse, because the hospital's full up, and Mrs. Anstruther's needed at home. Would you be able to give him tea presently?"

Georgie nodded. She, who had sat on the head of a ferocious horse straight from the realms of nightmare, could surely manage to give a man tea!

"Right you are, then. I'll be off. Lucky for us all you're

24

a born nurse," said the doctor, and he hastened out to his car, Mrs. Anstruther loping after him.

Georgie went thoughtfully downstairs. A born nurse? She had never pictured herself filling any really useful rôle in life. Dr. Warnford and Mrs. Jones did not know how terrified she had been—and was still, when she saw how pale her stranger looked.

He managed to smile, however, when she went into the room.

"I can never really thank you," he said. "I'd no idea you were such a kid —"

"A *kid*? I'm thirteen! Would you like some tea?"

"Yes, please, and then could you ring up the White Hart at Periton? That's where I'm staying. Tell them about Firefly."

"Does he belong to them, then?"

"No, rather not. He belongs to my aunt. She lent him to me, and I brought him down for the week-end. I used to know the moor pretty well, so I took him out rather too far, and night came on. My aunt'll never forgive me. But for you, he'd have had to be shot."

"Well, he's going to be all right," she said; "and soon Mother and the boys will be home, and you'll be looked after properly."

"You're looking after me as well as anyone could. . . . I say, I wish you could go to my aunt's school! You're just the sort of girl she wants—"

Georgie escaped. If his aunt wanted her pupils to sit on horses' heads, it must be a strange kind of school!

She made some tea, and then thought of Firefly. She dared not open the garage door, but she found some apples and the toasting-fork, and managed to feed him through the small window. Now she could see him clearly for the first time. Last night he had seemed as big as an elephant, and black as ink. Now she saw that he was really just a large edition of the ponies she loved to see wandering round the moors at Pencarne, and his satiny coat was brown. He ate the apples politely, though he had probably never been fed by toasting-fork before.

The stranger, who told her that his name was John

Primrose, was in great pain. He had fractured his collar-bone and strained his leg. He referred several times to his aunt, for he was talking a great deal, half feverishly, and she pictured a strong-minded lady of sixty or so, with grey hair, pince-nez, and a will of iron.

"Do you like her?" she asked. " We don't like our Aunt Milly much."

"Like?" he echoed. "My aunt's terrific. If you go to her school, you'll see . . ."

She visualized an old-fashioned establishment where one had to speak French at meals and walk in a crocodile, and where only the naturally good people, like Gerry, would keep out of trouble.

"I'd hate to go to boarding-school. One might as well be in prison."

"Prison? The Grange? That's a good one!" He smiled. "You like animals, and there are plenty of those about."

"Oh, yes, I love animals," she conceded, thinking of King Toby and the pups.

To her great relief, she heard the car turning in at the gate. Now for explanations! She ran to meet her mother, only to find that Dr. Warnford had stopped her in the village a few minutes ago, and had told her the whole story.

"Oh, darling, I shall never forgive myself for leaving you! I might have known. Let me see this poor man at once," and Mrs. Kane hastened into the house.

"Don't put the car in the garage," Georgie called after her. "There's a horse in it."

"Oh, Georgie, how *just* like you!" said Gerry. "It was a gorgeous party. You never saw such a spread—"

"I've brought you some of the stuff, Georgie. Afraid the trifle's wobbled a bit," said Rough, producing an untidy parcel.

"Let's go in," said Peter, smiling at his sister. "I want to hear the full story of last night's work."

She nodded and clung quite unashamedly to his hand. The reaction was setting in at last. She found that she was trembling, and very glad to sit quietly in Peter's bed-sitting-room, and listen to his concise account of the party. She

26

could not eat the food which Rough had kindly brought for her.

"I was so scared!" she burst out suddenly.

"I should say you were," Peter agreed, without surprise; "but you did it, that's the main thing. Well, as I was saying, Uncle Archie got on his hind-legs and held forth for forty-eight minutes—Tough timed him. And that reminds me, the Great-Grandies asked me to give you this. We've each got one, in case you didn't notice."

It was a lovely gold wristlet watch, inscribed with her initials and the date.

"Now," she said, when she had finished admiring it, "I *can't* ever forget yesterday, even if I want to: the Great-Grandies' 'do'; and my one-and-only adventure."

"You'll have heaps more," Peter prophesied, but she shook her head in a determined way.

"No, thank you. I don't like them. I've decided to live a very quiet life. You and the Lads will go out into the world and do things, but I'll always stay at home, and—and learn to cook, and all that sort of thing."

Peter looked at her and laughed.

"'Sweet Stay-at-Home'," he quoted. "You don't want to be like that, do you?"

She hesitated, for she too knew the poem.

"I don't want to be like the end bit—'Not for the knowledge in thy mind'. Just as if she couldn't have knowledge, even if she did stay at home."

"One needs real life as well as books, my good girl," he cried, in amused exasperation. "I realized that, I can tell you, when I first got smashed up and thought I shouldn't get about again."

"Yes, but, Peter, you're good at it, and I'm not."

"Good at what?"

"Life," she said, and her eyes filled with tears. "You and the Lads and Gerry—you can all do things well. You know what to do, and I don't. You'd have—sat on that awful horse's head—without being scared to death—"

She fled to her own room and banged the door. Peter sat looking thoughtful for a while, and then went downstairs to find his mother. She was just giving John Primrose his lunch, for no nurse had been forthcoming, and she had undertaken to look after him until he could travel back to Periton.

"What's wrong, Peter?"

"Nothing really, Mother. But if Dr. Warnford's coming soon, I think he ought to have a look at Georgie."

"Why?" Mrs. Kane asked in alarm. "Is her cold worse?"

"No, it isn't her cold." Peter paused, a sense of loyalty to his sister preventing him from saying that her nerves seemed unstrung. "She's a bit off colour, that's all."

"No wonder," John Primrose put in, from the couch. "She's a Trojan, that girl of yours, Mrs. Kane. I only wish you'd send her to the Grange—my aunt's starting a school, you know, and she's very keen to get the right type of girl. . . ."

Peter and his mother exchanged glances.

"Tell me about it," she said, while the visitor fed himself, rather shakily, with his left hand.

Peter turned away abruptly. He wondered if he had betrayed Georgie, who would, he thought, have a poor time of it if she did go away to school.

CHAPTER THREE

SHOCKS

"THERE'S something in the wind," Gerry said mysteriously, when they went to bed that night. "Auntie was talking to Dr. Warnford for simply ages in the hall. He said, 'It would be the very best thing if your husband agrees to it,' and Auntie said, 'Oh, he does: he's always wanted her to go, but I've been the stumbling-block.' What do you think of *that?*" she demanded.

"I think you were a pig to listen," said Georgie.

"I didn't! I was tidying the hall cupboard, and they both knew I was there. I coughed, too," said Gerry indignantly.

"Sorry," Georgie muttered, just as Mrs. Kane came in to say good-night.

"Auntie," said Gerry, in her meekest voice, "are we still going to Driscoe to-morrow to buy shoes for Rough and Tough?"

"No, dear, I'm afraid I'd forgotten we'd arranged that," Mrs. Kane answered abstractedly. "We can go another day. To-morrow I'm driving Mr. Primrose back to Periton—that's not very far from here, of course, but afterwards I'm going on to Dorset."

"Dorset?" cried two astonished voices.

"Yes, on business," said Mrs. Kane. "You know Aunt Milly's sister Kate lives near Bournemouth? I shall spend the night with her."

"*There!*" said Gerry, when she and Georgie were alone again. "There *is* something up her sleeve!"

"Well, it's her sleeve—not ours!" snapped Georgie, because a horrid little tickle of foreboding was creeping down her spine.

Mr. Jones, the vet, arrived before breakfast to take Firefly away in his van. The twins were sorry, because they liked having a horse in the garage, but Georgie was relieved to see the last of him. Mr. Primrose, looking much better now, with his arm strapped up, thanked her again most heartily as he said good-bye.

He and Mrs. Kane drove away quite early, and Georgie, Gerry, and the boys had a happy, peaceful day. They went for a walk in the frosty sunshine, and the twins amused themselves by training the puppies. Tough had given Velvet to Rough for Christmas, and Rough had given Plush to Tough.

"They're born retrievers," Rough said now. "Seems a pity we can't take them to school."

"Some schools allow pets," said Georgie. "St. John's is behind the times! Mr. Primrose's grim old aunt has animals at her school, because he said she was keen on them. Her one good point, I should think!"

29

Peter looked at her and frowned. ("Don't tell her," their mother had said. "It may not be suitable, and Miss Primrose probably can't take her at such short notice, whatever her nephew may say. Don't upset her till we know." And he had promised, so his lips were sealed.)

She saw his worried look, and thought he was tired. She suggested turning back with him, while the others went on to the village to ask how Lily Duncan was faring.

"I must put the potatoes on," she said importantly, as they went into the house. "Oh, cheers! Here's a letter from Daddy, and it's for me this time."

Mr. Kane, a hydraulic engineer, was in Africa at present, supervising the building of a great dam. His letters were always interesting, especially as they were never joint letters, but addressed to each member of the family in turn.

Georgie scanned the pages swiftly.

"He hopes I'll get on well next term—oh, dear, I must try! He says it's boiling hot, of course. . . . Oh, he's staying with a native chief! Think of Daddy in a mud hut, eating goodness knows what—I hope they're not cannibals! What *would* he do? Pretend to be a vegetarian, I suppose. . . . Peter, just listen to this!

I'm having a real adventure now. A small boy, black as ebony, tumbled into the river yesterday, and I fished him out. He turned out to be the son and heir of N'wambo, a great personage in these parts, who came in person to thank me—quite unnecessarily, for what else could one do? He offered me hospitality, which I was inclined to refuse; but after all it's a chance to see something of the real Africa; and, besides, he is a friendly and most enlightened man. So I accepted, and here I am, sitting on a straw mat in the shade of big trees which his ancestors planted, scribbling away with the fountain-pen which you and the boys gave me before I sailed. Will you ask Mother to let you get two more just like it—one for N'wambo, and one for the boy, whose name sounds like TTTTKKK. There is a daughter, now in England, studying to be a doctor.

30

N'wambo is learning English, and is most interested in my family.

Georgie passed the letter to Peter.

"Dear old Daddy. He makes light of it, but I bet there were crocodiles. Fancy N'wambo and TTTTKKK wanting pens—I should have thought they'd prefer bead necklaces."

"So should I," said Peter. "So would most Sweet Stay-at-Homes. But Daddy's on the spot, so he *knows*."

Mrs. Kane came home the following afternoon, and when she had had some tea, and read the African letter, and told them briefly about their Aunt Kate's pretty little cottage in the pine country, she asked Georgie to come upstairs with her. She looked grave, and Georgie wondered if anything could be wrong. Her mother took her into her bedroom, and handed her a small parcel.

"A present, Mother? Have you got them for everyone?" she asked, unwrapping the tissue paper.

"No, Georgie. It's not exactly a present. It's a hatband," said Mrs. Kane.

Georgie was surprised. "My school hat's fairly new."

"My dear, you're not going back to the High School. We've always thought you'd do better in a smaller school, and Daddy's been saying for years that you ought to be a boarder. So you're going to the Grange next term. It's a lovely school, Georgie, in a beautiful little village called High Lennet, on the Dorset-Hampshire border. It's a very old house," said Mrs. Kane, glancing uneasily at her stricken daughter. "It was once besieged by Roundheads, and—"

"But, *Mother!* The Grange! That's Mr. Primrose's hateful old aunt's school! I won't go!" raged Georgie.

"Hush, darling! It's for your own good. He described it to me, you see, and told me something of his aunt's methods, and I decided to go and see for myself. Don't sit there looking like the Sphinx!" Mrs. Kane exclaimed in natural irritation. "One would think you were being sent to a Jane Eyre establishment, instead of to a lovely place

31

where you'll have fresh air, and games, and horses to ride—"

"*Horses?*" Georgie repeated, with stiff lips.

"Yes. I saw some of them. The Grange has been a riding-school for some years, but Miss Primrose—who took her degree before she began teaching riding—has been asked by so many people to look after their daughters, that she decided to open a real school as well. This is to be the first term."

"But, Mother, you haven't given notice at the High School!" cried Georgie, seizing a forlorn hope.

"I know, but that can't be helped. Dr. Warnford thinks, and so do I, that you've stayed at home too long looking after Peter, and it's time you had a life of your own. So you're going to the Grange on the twenty-first of this month, and," said Mrs. Kane, "I know you'll like it when you get there."

Georgie gave a short laugh.

"Did you like your schooldays, Mother?"

Now Mrs. Kane had been sent to a strict, old-fashioned school kept by two grim, unimaginative sisters whom her grandmother had known in their youth. Georgie had often listened to tales of those unhappy days—the recollection of that time had been Mrs. Kane's chief reason for urging her husband to keep Georgie at home.

She wished now that Georgie's memory were not so good.

"The Grange School is entirely different from Laurel Villa," she said, "and I'm sure Miss Primrose is not in the least like the Misses Bitten. Laurel Villa was out-of-date even in my time, twenty years ago."

"Didn't you see Miss Primrose?" asked Georgie.

"No, she's away. I saw her secretary, Miss Eversley, and she showed me round. Miss Primrose will be back to-morrow, and I promised to telephone to her to confirm the arrangements."

This sounded so final that Georgie gave a despairing groan. Her mother tried to think of some consolation.

"You can take King Toby if you like—the girls may have pets—and you'll love the riding—"

32

"I don't want to ride—I *hate* horses!"

"Georgie! You always feed the ponies at Pencarne, and remember how upset you were over *Black Beauty*, and how you helped Firefly the other night—"

"I don't like them to be hurt, that's all," growled Georgie. "I don't like killing mosquitoes, but that doesn't mean that I want to live with them, in a swamp! The ponies are small, but big horses scare me to death."

"Well, you needn't ride," Mrs. Kane said wearily. "No one will force you. But remember how happy most girls are at boarding-school. Look at Gerry—"

But that was too much. With one last reproachful look, Georgie dashed out of the room and down the stairs. In the hall she met Peter, and saw his anxious glance.

"So you know, do you?" she fired at him. "You're in the plot! Oh, Peter, we were so happy—why must I go away?" She glared at the hat-band, which she had unconsciously brought down with her. It was a piece of plain corded green ribbon, with a small crest attached, bearing the letter "G" in gold. She flung it down, and stamped on it.

"Don't be an ass!" Peter stooped with some difficulty, and picked it up. "What's wrong with it? It's neat—"

"G for the Grange! Branding us like sheep! The High School badge is simply the Driscoe coat of arms. Oh, Peter, I felt there was something going on, but I didn't think of this." . . .

Angry tears started to Georgie's eyes, but she blinked them away because she heard Gerry coming.

"G," mused Peter, studying the hat-band. "A lucky omen, I think. G for Georgia. The Grange will be just your cup of tea."

"What's the meeting in aid of?" asked Gerry curiously.

"My new school." Georgie held up the crumpled ribbon.

"Bearding-school?" gasped Gerry. "So *that's* what was in the wind. . . . My hat, you'll have to watch your step! We had a new girl last term who wasn't half as untidy as you, but Matron simply chivvied her all day long.

33

One morning she had to make her bed five times—"

"Ever read the Book of Job, Gerry?" asked Peter. "There are three people in it who are rather like you," he said pleasantly, and she flushed.

"I'm *not* a Job's Comforter, Peter—I'm trying to help. You're jolly mean," she said indignantly, "always taking Georgie's part."

She was cross for the rest of the evening. Mrs. Kane was obviously depressed, and Georgie, pale and listless, sat in a corner pretending to read. The three boys played Rummy, but it was not much of a success. When Mrs. Kane suggested early bed, not one voice was raised in protest.

Georgie lay awake for hours, trying to picture the Grange. She liked old houses. Peter was interested in architecture and archæology, and had taught her a little of both. She liked history, too, and was excited at the thought of living in a house which had once been a Royalist stronghold. In a way, too, it was exciting to be going to a new school. It meant a fresh start, and if only there had not been all those horses to reckon with, she would have been really glad to go. She had failed at the High School, she knew. When she had first gone there, she had been the only new girl in a huge form, and had shrunk with such palpable dread from the inevitable teasing, that the girls had thought her a poor specimen, and had allowed her to remain "new". She had found a desk in an inconspicuous corner, and there she had stayed, dreaming her time away.

She realized now what a waste this had been. Perhaps her mother was right, and she *would* get on better in a smaller school. But those horses! She shuddered.

Once, when her family had been living in London, her nurse had taken her down some back streets and had stood chatting to a friend, while the small Georgie had wandered on ahead. And two enormous grey horses, harnessed to a dray, had taken fright at something and bolted towards her, and she, too terrified to move, had been nearly pinned against a wall. The nurse, knowing that she should not have brought the child to this place,

34

made her promise not to tell, and Georgie had kept her word. She had almost forgotten the incident, and really did not connect it with the terror she felt nowadays.

She slept badly, and had a headache next morning; but she possessed that pride that sometimes does instead of courage, and she made no further appeal.

She came down to find the others groaning with dismay.

"What's happened *now?*" she asked apprehensively.

"Mummy's told us that Uncle Archie and Aunt Milly are coming over to see us the day after to-morrow," sighed Tough.

"Please be quiet, all of you!" said Mrs. Kane. "Uncle Archie may be a little trying, but he *is* my cousin after all, and he was good to Uncle Dick and me when we were were small. He was so disappointed not to see Georgie at the party."

Georgie made a face. Uncle Archie—boastful, talkative, and too fond of practical jokes—had long ago singled her out for his especial favour. He and Aunt Milly had no children of their own, and were really fond of young people; but their fondness took an uncomfortable form.

"Uncle Archie's little petsy-wetsy!" said Rough, tweaking her short curly hair.

The visit of Uncle Archie and Aunt Milly was just as difficult as they had feared it would be. He was one of those people who instinctively find the least welcome topic of conversation, and proceed to worry it to death. He greeted Georgie with a bear-like hug.

"Well, well, Curly-locks! What's all this I hear?" he cried boisterously (yes, he really did talk like that). "Off to boarding-school, eh? Prunes and prisms and all that? Ah, Marcia, you could tell her a thing or two about Laurel Villa!" He ignored Mrs. Kane's frown. "Going to turn you into a horsewoman, are they? Your mother told the Great-Grandies in her letter. She says some of the girls will keep their own mounts."

"They can all keep pets," said Mrs. Kane.

"Well, well, we'll have to find our Curly-locks an Arab steed. Perhaps Kate woul spare Penelope—eh, Milly?"

Aunt Milly, who was small and timid, gave a nervous

35

little giggle. The Kanes waited for the joke to be explained, but Uncle Archie went on:

"Here are some stamped addressed envelopes, Georgie. If you're not happy—if they punish you as your mother used to be punished—just send word to your old uncle."

"Really, Archie, it's not necessary. Don't put ideas into her head. She knows that Laurel Villas don't exist nowadays," said Mrs. Kane, trying to hide her annoyance.

"If you don't get enough to eat, dearie," whispered Aunt Milly. "I can always send you a little something—"

"*We* don't get enough to eat!" said Tough, but nobody believed this statement.

"Well, cheery-bye, Curly-locks!" said Uncle Archie, just as they were departing; "and if a horse-box does draw up at the Grange one day, don't be surprised."

"Come and see the travelling-box we've made for Toby," said Rough, dragging his seething sister into the garden. Toby was purring by the fire, unaware that his mistress had decided to take him to school, too.

"Rough, you don't think he *will* send me an Arab steed?"

"No fear! Horses cost the earth to buy, and he's not very rich, you know. I'd no idea Aunt Kate had one—had you?"

Georgie shook her head, and forgot about the mysterious Penelope as she inspected King Toby's royal coach. The twins had cleverly converted a wooden tomato-basket for him.

"Glad you like it. I say, I hope Toby won't yowl all the way," said Rough. "It's more than possible that some of our people will get into the train."

He and Tough were returning to their school on the day that she was going to the Grange, and the three would be travelling together as far as Fontayne Junction, which was only two stations away from Lennet Magna.

"Toby and I won't disgrace you," she promised.

All the same, when the last evening came, it was very hard not to cry. Four trunks stood in the hall, strapped and labelled for Gerry was returning to St. Monica's on the twenty-second, and had characteristically got all her packing done beforehand. Four suitcases, one brand new, stood on top of the trunks, with Gerry's hockey stick and the twins' football beside them.

King Toby examined the luggage with suspicion.

"All cats hate comings and goings," said Mrs. Kanc, in extremely low spirits herself; and Georgie looked at her.

"Will he hate leaving home? He loves this house," she said and fought a silent battle with herself. "Mother, I won't take him. He'll be happier with you and Peter and the pups."

"Good for you," said Tough.

"I'll take the box, though," she said, in quick gratitude. "I can keep my junk in it.'

"One doesn't *have* junk at school, said Gerry."

In a way, Georgie was relieved when the fatal day dawned. She couldn't eat her breakfast, and saw to her surprise that the twins found some difficulty in swallowing theirs. They liked their school, which was in Somerset, but did not enjoy the actual moment of leaving home.

Mrs. Kane drove the three children and their luggage to Driscoe station. The train came in, and soon she and the twins were steaming out of the familiar station.

They were all very silent, the boys engrossed in comics. But when they reached Fontayne, where the blue caps of St. John's were very much in evidence, the twins leapt out joyfully.

"'Bye, Georgie—all the best!" they said blithely, and rushed up to a young master. "Hallo, sir! Did you have a good Christmas?"

Georgie felt very lonely. Lennet Magna was the next station but one, and a car would be waiting to meet the train and take her to High Lennet, which had no station of its own.

There was a long delay at the junction. She saw the St. John's boys march away to catch another train. Then an old lady came hurrying on to the platform, and somehow tripped over her umbrella. She fell down and upset her shopping basket, and apples and oranges rolled in all directions.

Obeying her natural instinct, Georgie jumped out of the train and ran to help. She picked up the old lady first, and took her to a platform seat. Then she collected the fruit and groceries, and was just handing them to their owner when—the engine whistled, and the guard waved his green flag.

She turned to run, but the old lady clung to her sleeve.

"Never risk it, me deurr! My nevvy broke his leg that way!"

In speechless horror Georgie watched the train gather speed. Not only had she lost it, but she had lost her luggage as well! The school car would wait in vain at Lennet Magna. She could hardly have made a worse beginning.

"Where do you want to go, missie?" asked the station-master, seeing her expression. "Lennet Magna? There'll be a local train along in an hour."

"Never mind, me deurr!" said the old lady. "You lost it through the kindness of your heart, and you shan't lose by it. Look!" and she handed the wretched Georgie a large red apple.

She bustled off to catch her own train, and Georgie ate the apple and wondered what Miss Primrose would say to her. Luckily, her ticket was in her pocket; but everything else had gone. It was turning cold, so she went into the waiting-room, and found a tabby cat in the act of pouncing on a mouse!

Georgie was experienced in this kind of thing, for Toby was an enthusiastic sportsman—indeed, his attitude towards mice was the one subject upon which he and she disagreed. She drove the cat away and rescued the mouse, which was not injured though terribly frightened. She found an old paper bag and put him into it.

"So I'm taking a pet to school, after all!" she thought.

Presently the stationmaster put his head round the door.

"Train's signalled, missie. That a 'G' on your hat?

38

You'll be going to the Grange, then. Come along," he said kindly.

Georgie and the mouse were soon on their way to Lennet Magna. He was a pretty little fellow, and she decided to call him Erasmus. She was quite glad of his company.

There was no car at Lennet Magna station, so she asked a porter the way to the Grange. He said it was two miles to the north, across a common, so she set off on foot.

They crossed the bridge in single file.

It was a beautiful common and very wild, reminding her of the moors at home. A stream ran through it, and was spanned by an old stone bridge. Just as she was about to cross, she heard the sound of hooves, and stood still while three people cantered towards her.

They crossed the bridge in single file. She must have looked as lost and frightened as she felt, for the foremost rider, a girl of sixteen or so, called out to her.

"You're for the Grange, aren't you?"

"Yes—worse luck!" said Georgie.

The girl raised her eyebrows, and the third rider, who seemed a few years older, moved involuntarily.

"Oh, you'll like it when you get there," the strange girl said, in some embarrassment.

"It's all right for *you*," Georgie said bitterly. "I suppose these horses come from there, as it's a riding-school as well. But *I've* got to be a boarder! I wish you'd tell me what Miss Primrose is like. I picture her very tough and leathery, with short grey hair like a man's, and gimlet eyes, and a cruel jaw."

It was unusual for Georgie to be so talkative with strangers—so unusual that she listened to herself with surprise. But nevousness tends to make people garrulous, and she really hardly knew what she was saying.

The first rider did not reply to this, though she and the girl behind her, who was obviously her sister, looked horror-stricken. But the other, the eldest of the trio, who was riding a beautiful bay, moved forward a few steps.

"I think," she said in a low, clear voice, "that you must be Georgia Kane. How is it that you're walking to the school?"

Georgie gasped something, and backed away, trembling at the scrutiny of those level blue eyes.

"You can't be—*Miss Primrose?*" she faltered.

The other smiled. She was quite young and very slender, with dark hair just showing under her bowler.

"But I am," she said, patting her horse as he side-stepped a little. "The school is half-a-mile farther on. You'll see some big gates. Go quickly, please. Matron will be anxious."

"But you *can't* be Miss Primrose!" Georgie burst out. "You're younger than your own nephew!"

"We can go into that later," said Miss Primrose, a glint of amusement in her eyes. "Now we must finish our ride, and you must go to the Grange. Good-bye for the present, Georgia!"

They trotted off across the common, and broke into a canter again. Georgie watched them in the soft, misty light, and then plodded on. She had been rude. Miss Primrose would tell her so before long. Those two girls had been scandalized. She blushed as she thought of what she had said.

The ground was rising now, and a village was looming ahead. But before she came to it, she saw some big white gates with "The Grange" printed across them. There was a little gate at the side, and she opened it with shaking hands, feeling that now indeed she was to be thrown to the lions.

But someone was waiting on the drive, an elderly woman in nurse's uniform, with a kind, humorous face. When she saw Georgia she smiled with a mixture of friendliness and relief.

"Georgia, isn't it? I'm the matron, as you can guess. Come in at once, my dear child: you must be starved."

"I—I'm sorry—"

"Because you're late? Never mind, we know all about that. The stationmaster telephoned us that you had caught the local train, but there wasn't time to send the car back. Come along," said Matron. "The main thing is that you've got here."

They walked up the drive together, and as they rounded a bend Georgie had her first glimpse of the house.

CHAPTER FOUR

TEEPOO

IT was a very large house, but not too large to be a home. Originally built in Elizabethan days, it had been altered and enlarged during the centuries so that now it was in the shape of an E without the middle bar. In the left wing, Georgie saw the square, exquisite architecture of Queen Anne, but the right wing seemed much more modern.

The drive ended in a circle in front of the stout oaken

41

door. Four stone steps led up to this, and on either side of them crouched a stone lion. She touched one shyly as she passed, with Matron leading the way.

"Funny!" she said. "I was thinking of lions just now."

"Lions?" said Matron.

"Yes. I felt a bit like Daniel," said Georgie.

Matron turned to smile at her.

"Well, I hope you will be like him," she said. "He was undaunted, wasn't he? And he had his reward. Now, my dear, it's three o'clock, and I'm afraid you've had no lunch. Those girls who have already arrived are unpacking now, so I think you'd better have something on a tray in my room."

Georgie, completely dazed by this time, could not even answer, but followed her through a great panelled hall and up a flight of shallow oak stairs. A maid passed them on the landing, and smiled in a welcoming way. Georgie tried to smile back, but her face was stiff.

From another part of the house she could hear gay voices and the quick patter of feet. She shivered.

"How—how many girls are there?" she faltered.

"Twelve have arrived so far. There'll be only thirty, all told, this term," Matron explained, as she took her into a a small room where a wood fire was burning cheerfully. "Miss Primrose wants to start the school gradually. Quite a number will be arriving next term, and when September comes, and the real school year begins, there will be a nice crowd."

Georgie did not know whether to be glad or sorry that the school was to be so small this term. The fewer the better, in one way, she thought, and yet she hated being conspicuous.

"I've lost my luggage," she said forlornly.

"Oh, no, you haven't—it's in your room," said Matron. "The car fetched that, if it couldn't fetch you. You can unpack presently. Now you must have a meal."

She disappeared, and presently came back, carrying a tray, and accompanied by a sturdy red-haired girl of about Georgie's own age.

"This is Susan Walker. Georgia Kane. Susan has just

arrived," Matron told Georgie, "and her father, who's driven her all the way from London, says she's had nothing but sandwiches."

Susan laughed. She did not seem to be in the least shy.

"Awful ones they were, too," she said, in a deep voice. "We wanted to give them to the ponies in the New Forest, but they didn't show up. This looks good!"

Matron had brought bowls of soup, little meat patties, and plates of fruit and junket. Susan fell to with gusto. Georgie struggled with her soup, envying her assured companion.

"Now I must go downstairs again," Matron announced, "so I'll leave you two together. You'll be sleeping in the same room—Number Eight. I think you can find your way—straight along this passage, up the two stairs, and turn to your right."

She hurried away, and Susan looked at Georgie.

"Aren't you hungry? Sure? Well, can I have your patty then? I'm ravenous! I always am. . . ."

"Do you know Miss Primrose?" Georgie asked, feeling that she must be a family friend.

"Not yet," said Susan. "Mummy knew her mother, though—that's why I'm here. It's fun, I think, seeing a school start. Have you been to the stables yet? I'm dying to go. Black Agnes arrived yesterday, and I've simply got to see how she likes it."

"Black Agnes? That was Mary, Queen of Scot's palfrey," said Georgie, interested at last.

"Who's she? Someone in history—but I never could sort out all the Marys and Richards and things," returned Susan, munching hard. "Oh, now I know—she had her head chopped off: we saw her in Madame Tussaud's. So that's why my Uncle James called her Black Agnes—he's a great historican, or whatever you call it!"

"Historian." Georgie thought this the most ignorant girl she had ever met.

"Historian," repeated Susan, not at all abashed. "I knew it was something like that. Look here, I'm not being a hog, but—aren't you going to eat your junket?"

. . . feeding a very oddly-marked skewbald.

Georgie passed her the plate in disgusted silence. Susan saw her face, and burst out laughing.

"I know I'm awful. That," she said simply, "is why I've been sent to school."

"Haven't you ever been before?"

"Oh, yes—to sixteen! And that's as bad as none, because as soon as I started to learn anything, I was whisked away. Daddy studies dialects, you see—he writes books about them, and of course he's got to sample them all. Mummy and I always went with him until just lately. We spent Christmas with Uncle James, and he told them I was an igg—igger—*you* know."

"Ignoramus," said Georgie, heartily agreeing with Uncle James.

"That's it. Just what I was going to say. Well, here I am, complete with Black Aggie." Susan devoured the remainder of her bread roll.

"Don't you feel—homesick?" asked Georgie.

"Of course. But what's the use of saying so? Come on, let's find the stables."

"But Matron said—"

"Oh, phooey! We can unpack later," said Susan.

Georgie followed her, not because she wanted to, but because she could not face the other girls in the bedroom alone. They went downstairs and out into the garden. A young man dressed as a groom passed them, and they asked him the way.

"I'm going there now," he said: "I'll show you."

The stables were much larger than Georgie had expected. They were, in fact, three quite big buildings, and a clock-tower which she had seen from Matron's window was built on to the roof of the middle one.

"Where's Black Agnes?" Susan asked the groom.

"In A Block, miss. This way. There's some other young ladies in there, too," he said.

This was the middle building. They went inside, and Georgie's heart beat fast when she saw the row of horses and ponies in their loose boxes, all turning round to look at them. Two girls, one about seventeen, and the other a little younger than Georgie and Susan, were feeding a very oddly-marked skewbald, whose face had a cheerful, almost humorous expression.

"Hallo!" said the elder girl. "I'm Ruth Conway and this is my sister Anne. How do you like Pierrot?"

"Angel!" said Susan, patting his neck. "I'm Susan Walker, by the way, and she's Georgia somebody. . . . What's the matter, Georgia? Come and speak to him. I'm going to see Aggie, she's over there, at the end."

"Yes, come and say 'Hallo' to Pierrot," said Anne, smiling at the shrinking Georgie. "He's Ruth's really, but she lets me ride him. Here's an apple—like to give it him?"

She had short, crisp brown hair, and laughing brown eyes. Georgie warmed towards her, and took the proffered apple.

"Here you are," she said to Pierrot, wishing she had a toasting fork. He bent to nibble it, and at that moment she dropped her paper bag, and Erasmus escaped.

He ran up and down the straw by Pierrot's legs, and then swarmed up the manger. Pierrot saw him, and reared wildly, whinnying in terror. The horse in the next box caught his panic and did the same. Ruth dragged Georgie back, or she might have been struck by one of those hooves, and a groom came running up.

"It's a mouse!" said Anne. "There, there, old boy—it's gone now. All right, Pierrot!" She looked at Georgie in surprise. "Don't you know that horses are frightened of mice?"

"You never been and brought one in, miss?" asked the groom.

"Yes, I did!" said Georgie, goaded into defiance. "He's my mouse, and I want him, and—you don't seem to think that mice may be frightened of horses!"

"What's going on in here?" drawled a new voice behind them. "Mice? Don't say this kid brought one with her?"

"Yes, but I don't think she knew, Barbara," said Ruth. "It's all right now—they're calming down. There's your mouse, Georgia—sitting down just behind Pierrot. Can you get it without his seeing?"

"I'll get it, miss," said the groom, and he did so,

46

deftly. Georgie took Erasmus from him, holding him carefully in both hands, and as she turned away, feeling in disgrace, she heard the girl they called Barbara laughing softly.

"What a queer kid! Did you see how she shrank back? Anyone would think she's *afraid* of horses. . . ."

Susan came back now, quite oblivious of the mouse episode.

"Aggie's fine," she said happily. "Just a bit frisky, perhaps—she nearly knocked me down! Come and see her, Georgia."

But Georgia had had enough of the equine race. She fairly ran out of the stables, and Barbara's mocking laugh came floating after her.

Now she was to see Matron in another guise.

"Georgia—where's Susan? I thought I told you both to go to bedroom Eight. Fetch her at once, please," said Matron, not at all pleased at having to come out to the stables to find her errant charges.

"Susan—we've got to unpack," called Georgie.

"Coming!" was the blithe reply. "But have you seen Rockie? He's Miss Primrose's own horse, and the loveliest—"

"Susan Walker!" said Matron, from the doorway.

"Er—coming!" said Susan, in a very different tone. And she came.

Matron took them to bedroom Eight, and opened the door. Two more girls looked up, from a welter of neatly-folded clothes. They were Brenda Deacon and Rosalie Hall, aged fourteen and thirteen respectively.

"This is your bed, Georgia," Brenda announced, after Matron had introduced them. "You're lucky, you've got a window."

"I thought there'd be dormitories," said Georgie, "with rows of little white beds. . . ."

"Oh, there couldn't be, could there?" said Rosalie. "None of the bedrooms here is very big. The girl next door has a tiny room—she's by herself." She giggled suddenly. "Go and ask her for—for a needle and cotton, will you?"

Brenda giggled too. "Yes, go on!"

"But I don't know her," Georgie objected, "and I don't *want* a needle!"

"Well, *I* do. Not shy, are you?" jeered Rosalie.

"I'll go," said Susan, good-natured as always.

"No, I will." Georgie would not be branded as a coward. She knew that for some reason these girls were trying to tease her—that they had already seen that she was timorous and silly, and so fair game. She knocked at the other door.

"Come in," said a slow voice, and she opened the door. Then she saw why they had played this trick. The girl who sat by the window, looking out at the garden, was as dark as a coal. . . .

It was a difficult moment for Georgie, but she kept her head. On no account must this girl think herself an oddity, to be stared at with vulgar curiosity. She put one hand behind her and surreptitiously tore at one of the pleats in her skirt.

"Excuse me. I'm Georgia Kane, from Number Eight, and I've torn my skirt. Have you—a needle and cotton?"

The other girl smiled, showing beautiful teeth. She was dressed in the correct Grange uniform. She wore her frizzy hair in a short bob.

"I—Teepoo," she said, in her slow, rather pleasant voice. "Yes. I have needle."

Her English was good, though scanty. She obviously understood everything that was said to her. She went to a work-box that was standing on her chest of drawers, and found the things for which Georgia had asked.

"I sew for you."

"Oh, no, thanks, I can do it. . . ." Georgie said wildly.

"You cannot sew own back," said Teepoo. Swiftly she repaired the burst pleat.

"Thanks awfully. Are you keen on horses?" asked Georgie, reflecting that, as everyone here seemed to be mad about them, this would be a good gambit.

"Keen?" said Teepoo.

"Do you like horses? Have you got one?"

48

"Yes and yes," said Teepoo. "But I not ride much. I here to work. You have pony of your own?"

"No!" said Georgia. Then, "Well, I must unpack—see you later!" and she went back to bedroom Eight.

Brenda and Rosalie were still speechless with giggles. Susan was unpacking, looking puzzled.

"Well?" spluttered Brenda, who had a sharp, foxy face.

"Well, she lent me the needle. She even mended my skirt for me," Georgie said coldly, and began to take the clothes out of her trunk.

"What's the joke?" asked Susan. "Stop cackling, you idiots!"

"Wait till you see her," said Rosalie. "She's black! Bet you got a shock, didn't you, Georgia?"

This was a joke, however, that Susan did not appreciate. Her green eyes flashed as she looked at Brenda and Rosalie.

"Stop it—she'll hear you laughing! Of all the rotten things, treating her as a *show!* Why shouldn't she be dark? You're as bad as the rude little boys who yell 'Ginger!' at me in the street. You're worse! She's just the same as the rest of us, and I'm going to tell her so!"

"Susan—don't!" cried Georgie. "You'll make her feel—"

But it was too late. Susan had already burst into Teepoo's room without knocking, and they could hear her addressing its occupant in stentorian tones.

"Hallo! I'm Susan Walker. How do you do? I know I'm going to like you. Isn't it funny, I've got a mare called Black Agnes!"

Georgie longed for an earthquake. As she followed Susan into the other room, she was relieved but astonished to hear Teepoo laugh.

"How you do? My pony called Spot."

To her own surprise, Georgie heard herself asking, "Why Spot?"

"English missionary near home, he has little dog called Spot. Good name," said Teepoo.

"Where *is* your home?" asked Georgie.

Teepoo told her.

"Why, that's where my father is! Building a dam—"

The negress stood up suddenly. She was taller than Georgie and Susan, and very slender and graceful.

"Your name?" she said. "I not hear first time."

"Kane. Georgia Kane."

"Then," said Teepoo, her eyes sparkling with delight, "my father, your father—friends. Your father save my little brother from river—"

"Oh, no, it isn't possible!" gasped Georgie, while Susan—and Brenda, Rosalie, and several other girls who were halfway into the room, too, by now—listened with goggling eyes. "Your brother must be TTTTKKK!"

How Teepoo laughed! Her laughter was so infectious that they all joined in, without the slightest trace of mockery.

"No, no! My brother called—" She made some strange sounds.

"But that's what I said: TTTTKKK. And you're the girl who's going to be a doctor? My father wrote and told us about you, and—and he's staying with your father now!" It cost Georgie something to say this, with all those girls looking on ready to giggle, but she was glad she had, for Susan squeezed her arm.

"We must have a talk about fathers soon. Yours seems as crazy as mine!" she said, and because she was Susan, the words were not offensive. "Meanwhile, come and finish your unpacking. I believe we've got to go to Miss Primrose or something. Oh, I do wish it was time for tea!"

Georgie had just finished unpacking—which, to her meant tipping everything out of trunk and suitcase, and stuffing clothes, books, and writing materials into the three drawers provided for her use—when Ruth Conway came to the door.

"Susan and Georgia, will you come down to Miss Primrose's study now? She wants to see each girl separately, and later on she's going to talk to us all together."

She led them through a maze of passages to a door which was labelled "Study".

"Anne and I came early this morning—that's how we

50

know our way about," she said, smiling. "Will one of you knock and go in?"

Georgie hung back as usual, so Susan went. She emerged ten minutes later, smiling broadly.

"Tuck-boxes *are* allowed," she said, in a stage whisper, "as long as we share out what's in them. I must write to Mummy at once! Go on, Georgia—she isn't a dragon really."

Georgie went into the study. Miss Primrose was sitting in an easy-chair by the fire, a large black cat purring by her feet. She motioned Georgie to another chair opposite her. She looked quite different now that she was not in riding-dress, but her blue eyes were as clear as Georgie remembered them to be, and her manner was just as informal.

"I hope you're settling down," she said. "The three other girls in your room are about your age, so I think you'll enjoy yourselves. This evening I'm going to explain the rules to you all, and tomorrow a typed copy of them will hang in every room. Miss Eversley, my secretary, has wired to your mother to say that you have arrived safely."

"Thank you, Miss Primrose."

The head-mistress smiled at her tense face.

"Don't you like horses?" she asked unexpectedly.

"N—not much. They're so big. I like cats and dogs, and—mice," said Georgie, thinking of Erasmus, now scrabbling about inside her suitcase. "I've got a mouse. May I keep him for a pet?"

"Yes, if you really want to. A tame one?"

"No. I found him in the waiting-room at Fontayne."

"Then don't you think," said Miss Primrose, "that he would enjoy himself much more if you let him loose in the vegetable garden? If you keep him, he will have to live in a cage, and I don't think he'd live very long."

"Then I *will* let him loose," said Georgie, secretly relieved. "It's all right as long as he's safe. There was a cat—I don't think I could get really wrapped up in a mouse."

Miss Primrose smiled. "It might be a little chilly, perhaps!" she suggested. "Well, Georgia. I expect you wonder why I asked you if you liked horses. Your mother told me in her last letter that you were very fond of all animals, but apt to be nervous, and said that you yourself should decide whether to learn riding or not. I never advise people to ride against their inclination, for the horse's sake as well as their own. I think you had better wait a week or two, and then come to me again. All the girls who do ride—and I think that means everybody except you, and little Nancy Andrews, one of the juniors who has been very ill—will be expected to help with the stable work. You won't be asked to do that, but if you'd like to offer, it would be a very good way of getting to understand horses."

"I don't mind feeding them," said Georgie generously.

Miss Primrose smiled again. "Maxwell, the head groom, has asked me to make it plain that girls are not required to do the actual feeding. It's such a temptation to give tit-bits, you see, and we can't have the horses becoming upset. He will give people apples and various little things to give them when they come back from a ride, but the grooms themselves do all the feeding, though they may be glad of experienced help in the preparation of the meals. You look surprised."

"I'm wondering what else there is to do, *but* feed them," Georgie owned, and this time Miss Primrose laughed outright.

"You'll see very soon that horses are most exacting people, and need an immense amount of care. They deserve it, too," she said. "They're wonderful friends to us, and we owe it to them to treat them with all possible consideration." She paused, and looked thoughtfully at Georgie. "I understand from your mother that you have spent a good deal of time with your invalid brother. The stationmaster at Fontayne said on the telephone that you had lost the train through helping an old lady. You yourself have told me that you brought a mouse with you because you thought a cat would get it. All this proves that you are good at looking after people. Will you help Miss Giles, the kindergarten mistress, with the six juniors?

52

And there's Teepoo, an African girl who has come for two terms, who may feel a little strange. . . ."

"I've met her already, Miss Primrose. Isn't it funny, my father has been staying with her people. I—I don't know if I'm much good at looking after strangers," Georgie said rather anxiously, "but I'll try."

"Good—that's all we *can* do, isn't it? Trying is the first step, always. Oh, and there's Pixie—one of the ponies who's gone lame. He's by himself in the sick quarters, and could do with a little petting. Ask Maxwell to show you where he is. Well, I think that's all, Georgia. The gong will sound for tea in a moment, and after that there will be a medical inspection. Dr. Lake from the village will come up to see you all. Those were his daughters you saw with me this afternoon," she added. "That bay I was riding is one they have just bought, and they asked me to try him out."

Georgie coloured as she rose from her chair.

"I'm afraid I was rude, Miss Primrose. I'm sorry. I didn't know it was you."

"But how could you know? Think no more about it, my dear. You wondered why I appear younger than my own nephew! It's quite simple really. My father married twice, and the John Primrose whom you helped so ably that frosty night is the son of my half-brother, who was grown up before I was born. My mother's parents left this house to me, and their horses too. Run along now," said Miss Primrose.

And Georgie ran, feeling that in her new headmistress she had a real friend. So she was not going to be forced to ride, after all! All she had been asked to do was keep an eye on Teepoo and the juniors. She had never had much to do with people younger than herself, so this last was a grave responsibility. Still, she would try. Miss Primrose had said that trying was the first step. Georgie had heard this maxim from her earliest days: she had met it in copy-books, and on poker-work calendars; but until now it had meant nothing at all.

A gong boomed in the hall below. Something cannoned into her violently, flinging her against the banisters.

"Tea!" shouted Susan Walker as she galloped noisily down the stairs.

CHAPTER FIVE

THE GRANGE

GEORGIE, recollecting tales of Laurel Villa, had expected long tables, doorstep bread-and-butter, and spasmodic conversation in halting French. In the refectory at the Grange, there were a number of little square tables, each laid for four people, and at the far end was a smaller table at which sat two of the staff. The elder of these (whom Georgie learned later was Miss Kennedy, the second mistress) said Grace, and after that conversation proceeded unchecked—and in English!

She found herself at a table with Susan, Teepoo, and Anne Conway. There were no "doorsteps", but plates of thin bread-and-butter, sandwiches, and cake. This time she could eat perfectly well, and soon felt much better. Anne was a gentle, friendly girl with plenty to say for herself, Teepoo was quiet, but answered readily when she was addressed, and Susan was too busy demolishing her tea to speak much. Georgie was able to take stock of the other girls for the first time.

She counted them. They were thirty altogether, so evidently all had arrived by this time. She glanced at the two junior tables, and saw that the small people there seemed perfectly at home with a young, jolly mistress who had caused much amusement by sitting on one of the small-sized chairs.

"They don't need looking after," thought Georgie, whose story-book mind had visualized six disconsolate and tearful infants. "And Teepoo seems to be getting on all right, too. That leaves Pixie—I'll have to concentrate on him."

After tea there was the promised medical inspection. Dr.

Lake was big and cheerful. He told Georgie that she was very fit, though she needed to put on more weight and develop her muscles.

"Still, riding will soon do that for you," he said. "Finest exercise in the world. My daughters have ridden with Miss Primrose for two years, and they're Amazons now."

Georgie gave a sickly smile and slipped away. She had no wish to be an Amazon.

When all the unpacking had been done, the girls were summoned to the big hall, which was part of the old building and a very beautiful room. There was a platform at one end, and Miss Primrose addressed the girls from here, with the rest of the staff around her. Georgie was surprised to see so many mistresses for so few girls. Used to the enormous forms at the High School, it seemed to her fantastic, until she remembered that the Grange would soon swell to three or four times its present size.

There was Miss Kennedy, tall, rather severe, and not very young. There was the pretty dark-haired French mistress, who was to be addressed as Miss Briac, and not Mademoiselle (later on, Georgie discovered why!). There was Miss Starr, the games mistress—another Amazon, Georgie thought with alarm. There was Miss Giles, the kindergarten mistress. There were also Miss Waite, who taught mathematics, Miss Dennis, who taught science, and Miss Moon, whose subjects were art and handicrafts.

"This is a very exciting moment for us all," said Miss Primrose. "Beginnings are always full of such wonderful possibilities. This is the first day of the Grange School, and we shall remember it all our lives. It's our school. It belongs to all the people in this room at the moment, and we have it in our power to make it a success. I don't want it to be just another boarding-school in the country. I want it to be a place which you will all look back upon with affection in after years. We shall have our ups and downs, of course. Sometimes you will think I am hard and unreasonable, and sometimes, no doubt, I shall wonder why I ever wanted to have a school at all—" there was a general laugh at this, in which she herself joined—"but if we have faith in one another, and honestly try to do our best, I believe we shall make a good school for ourselves, and for those who come after us. We have been trying," she continued, glancing at her staff, "to think of a motto, but so far we haven't succeeded. Miss Kennedy, who will take you for English, thinks that we can't do better than remember Miss Betsy Trotwood's words to David Copperfield, when she took him to school: 'Never be mean in anything; never be false; never be cruel. Avoid those three vices, and I can always be hopeful of you.' "

Susan dug Georgie in the ribs.

"Who's she talking about? Betsy Thingummy and David Whatisit?" she hissed.

"They're in a book. By Charles Dickens," Georgie hissed back.

"Oh, him—I thought he wrote for the films," returned Susan, regardless of Georgie's gasp of horror.

"No talking, please," said Miss Primrose. Her voice was still pleasant, but there was a sudden crispness in it which made all the girls involuntarily hold themselves a little straighter. "Now I'll just read you the form lists as they stand at present," she added, "and then you can do what you like until supper time."

She took a list from a table beside her, and began to read. "Sixth Form: Ruth Conway, Greta Davis, Janet Rose, and June Thurston. These four girls are our first prefects, and Ruth will be head of the school. Fifth Form: Mary James, Laura Kenton, Joy Thurston, and Teepoo. Fourth Form: Patience Best, Brenda Deacon, Rosalie Hall, Georgia Kane, Pamela Pinkerton, Barbara Snow, and Judy Thurston. Third Form: Anne Conway, Myfanwy Jones, Sally Norris, Susan Walker—"

Georgie lost interest after that, for the names of the juniors meant nothing to her. She looked at the girls who would be with her in the Fourth. Brenda and Rosalie she already knew—too well! Judy Thurston, the youngest of three tall, lean sisters, looked rather nice, she thought, but Patience Best, whose fair hair was scragged back in an uncompromising plait, and who actually wore black woollen mittens, seemed old-fashioned and prim in the extreme. Pamela Pinkerton must be this cheerful-looking person with very short black hair cut in a fringe. The sixth girl, Barbara Snow, met Georgie's interested gaze with an amused and insolent stare. She was what the Kane family always called "khaki-coloured"—eyes, hair, and even her skin having a curiously yellowish-brown tinge. Her manner was completely assured, something like Geraldine's; but Gerry, in her most superior mood, had never worn that little sneer. Georgie remembered that Barbara had been in the stable when Erasmus made his unwelcome appearance there.

When they left the hall, she sought out Matron and asked if she might let Erasmus loose in the garden. Matron agreed that this was a good idea, and lent her a torch.

Georgie was just letting herself out through a side door when Patience happened to pass.

"Are you going out?" she asked, in a precise little voice.

"No, I'm sitting by the fire!" Georgie retorted, falling for once into the language of Rough and Tough. But the sarcasm was lost on Patience, whose big blue eyes widened in surprise.

"But there's no fire out there! That leads into the garden," she said seriously.

Georgie felt rather ashamed of herself.

"I know. I was just being stupid. I'm going out to set my mouse free."

"I'll come with you, then," said Patience, "because you won't find your way in the dark. Shall I hold the torch?"

It was a very black night, and Georgie was grateful for the offer. She noticed that the other girl seemed to find her way with ease. They went to what was evidently a large kitchen-garden, and there Erasmus was ceremoniously released.

"We'll go back by the stables," said Patience. "It's not so creepy."

"Do you mind the dark, then?"

"I don't exactly *like* it. You see," Patience said unexpectedly, "there are lots of tales about this house. It used to be called 'Goblin Grange', only Miss Primrose

57

has dropped the Goblin part now, and our housekeeper told me that in her young days people wouldn't pass it in the dark."

Georgie shivered. "It doesn't *feel* spooky. . . . How do you know all this? Do you live in High Lennet?"

"In Lennet Magna. I live with my guardian there, and I've ridden with Miss Primrose for some time. Have you seen the ponies yet?"

"Not all of them. Have you one of your own?"

"Oh, no," said Patience: "my guardian isn't at all well off. It's very kind of him to send me here. He thought young companionship would be good for me, but I'm afraid he'll be lonely."

"Is he very old?" Georgie asked.

"He's ninety-three," said Patience, "and our house-keeper is eighty. We've led a *very* quiet life, and I'm afraid I shall find this youthful atmosphere extremely trying at first."

"I—I expect you will," Georgie agreed, thinking that here was someone even less well-suited to boarding-school than herself. "Do you play games?"

"Only cribbage and backgammon. . . . I suppose you do?"

"Hockey, netball, and tennis. But I'm no good at them," said Georgie, with a burst of candour. "And I can't ride at all, and I don't want to!"

"I love it, but I ride side-saddle. I'm afraid the girls will laugh," said Patience. "I shan't mind their laughing at *me*, but they mustn't laugh at Guardie."

A sudden sound made Georgie start and clutch at her companion.

"That's only Mademoiselle," said Patience reassuringly.

"Miss Briac?" gasped Georgie. "It sounded like a horse!"

Patience chuckled for the first time. "She *is* a horse—not Miss Briac: Miss Primrose's own beautiful mare, who's being trained by Maxwell, the head groom. She came from France and is called Mademoiselle. She's lovely. Of course we don't ride her—she has a separate stable and everything. But Maxwell will let you see her if

"Doesn't the house look wonderful?"

you ask. She's extremely highly strung, though, so he never lets one go too near."

Georgie thought that she would prefer to take Mademoiselle's beauty on trust.

"Miss Primrose's nephew may be going to ride her in the next point-to-point," Patience went on, "though I hear he met with an accident."

"Yes," said Georgie drily, "I heard that too. Oh, look, the moon's coming out—doesn't the house look wonderful?"

With one accord the girls stood still and looked at the vast mass ahead of them. With lights in nearly all the windows, and the tall Elizabethan chimneys thrown into high relief against the sky, it looked mysterious and very, very old. Georgie wondered how many times the moon had looked down upon it as it was looking now. Men in slashed doublets and plumed hats had stood by those doors; women in stiff brocade had waited by those windows. She pictured the house shuttered and barred as it must have been when the Royalists of long ago had defended it against Cromwell's men.

They were both silent as they went indoors, as if the Grange had laid a spell upon them. When they entered the big square room next to the hall, that was to be used as a common-room now, they heard Brenda Deacon holding forth to Barbara Snow:

"—so I said to Mother, 'Well, if I must go to school, I'd rather have a well-established one, with traditions and all that,' but she said I'd get more riding here, and of course it *is* a nice old place. I mean, it'll be quite good, afterwards, to say one's been here. . . ."

- "Oh, yes, I'm all for it," drawled Barbara; "and traditions are a bit of a bore, aren't they?"

"What *are* they, anyway?" demanded Susan. "I thought tradition was something you spread, and then got shot for doing it!"

"That's sedition," said Georgie. A little while ago she had despised Susan for her ignorance, but somehow her mind was already broadening. "Traditions are—well, it's rather hard to explain. Drake finishing his game of bowls with the Armada in sight, and Nelson at Trafalgar, and Guy Fawkes, and tossing pancakes on Shrove Tuesday, and Yule logs—all those things are part of English tradition."

"I see," said Susan vaguely.

"My country too—many traditions," said Teepoo, with sparkling eyes.

"That was quite well put, Georgia," said Ruth, who was sitting with two other prefects. "I think it's rather exciting to come to a new school, because we have to start making its traditions."

Georgie found herself pushed forward into a little group of girls, and realized that the room was divided into two factions—those who, like Ruth, saw the romance of their position, and those who agreed with Barbara that traditions were a bore.

"All this stuff about Nelson and pancakes!" sniffed Laura Kenton. "Sentimental cotton-wool! What *good* does it do? I'm glad this school isn't one of those places with famous old girls, and a spot railed off where the first netball was bounced!"

Everyone laughed at that.

"All the same," said Janet Rose, a tall girl who seemed to be very friendly with Ruth, "when my young sister, who's only four, comes to the Grange in about eight years' time, I'm pretty sure she'll be proud of the traditions it will have collected by then."

Barbara was trying in vain to think of more arguments. She looked rather spitefully at Georgie.

"You've made one already, anyway," she said. "Bringing a mouse into the stables, and scaring the horses out of their wits—it was too funny for words!"

"*Did* she?" crowed Brenda, and Georgie found herself blushing miserably.

"Yes, I did," she said. "I didn't know they'd mind. I don't know anything about horses."

Now they all looked at her in astonishment.

"Don't you ride?"

"Don't you *want* to?"

"Why on earth have you come to the Grange?"

The last question was fired by Barbara, and Georgie was trying to think of an answer when Rosalie chipped in:

"Don't you know? She's come to start our traditions for us: instead of St. George and the Dragon—Georgia and the Mouse!"

It was at this precise minute that Miss Eversley, the secretary, came in.

"Is Georgia Kane here? Georgia, your aunt, Mrs. Bevan, has just telephoned. Unfortunately the line was not very clear, and she rang off before I had got the message Do you know what she means about sending you a mount?"

A rustle of excitement ran round the room. Georgie was bewildered. Mrs. Bevan was Aunt Milly's sister Kate, and she remembered Uncle Archie's mysterious remark about "Penelope".

"Something was said, last holidays," she told Miss Eversley, "but I didn't take it seriously. She's not a real

61

aunt, you see. We hardly know her. I'd no idea that she really meant to send me a pony of my own."

"It's very awkward," said the secretary. "All the girls who want to bring their own horses have to let Miss Primrose know well in advance, and then proper provision can be made for them. Maxwell will be rather upset about this, as he's planned the stables for this term. What is Mrs. Bevan's telephone number?—she's not in the book."

"She isn't on the phone, Miss Eversley. She must have used a call-box. And I don't know her address," said Georgie, in despair. "Could I ring up Mother? She's stayed with Aunt Kate, so she must know where she lives."

Miss Eversley shook her head.

"I'm afraid that would be no use, Georgia. I did catch part of the message. The horse—or, rather, mare, as the name appears to be Penelope—is leaving early to-morrow morning and should arrive here at midday. . . ."

CHAPTER SIX

THE ARAB STEED

GEORGIE lay in her divan bed by the coveted window, listening to the regular breathing of Susan, Brenda, and Rosalie. She was very tired and longed to go to sleep herself, but she was quaking too much for that. She had formed a truly forbidding picture of Penelope—a creature if gigantic proportions, with rolling eyes, flared nostrils, and tremendous teeth . . . "An Arab steed," Uncle Archie had called her. She had no idea what an Arab steed was like—except that the poem, *The Arab's Farewell to his Horse*, had always made her eyes prick with tears.

Was it possible that she could become so attached to

Penelope that she could address such moving words to her? She thought not.

What a stir Miss Eversley's announcement had caused that evening in the common-room! The girls had been full of questions.

"No, I've no idea what she's like," Georgie had admitted, looking as dazed as she felt. "My uncle said she was an Arab."

And then they had all begun telling her how lucky she was, and she had not dared to ask what an Arab was like. Maxwell had come to the house to discuss arrangements with her. He was a keen-faced, grizzled man of sixty or so, bow-legged and weather-beaten.

"You're the young lady who wasn't going to ride," he said. "I reckon you'll look at things different now you've got your own horse—eh, miss?"

He had come into the common-room. All the girls could hear this conversation. Georgie, for all her fears was no coward. With vague thoughts of upholding the family honour, she looked him straight in the face.

"Oh, yes," she said firmly. "Of course I must learn now. I'm very sorry I couldn't let you know about Penelope before."

"That's all right, miss," he said genially. "It couldn't be helped, and I never blames folk for what can't be helped. We'll find room for her, never fear. It'll likely be the end box in Block A."

"Next to Black Aggie!" cried Susan, when Maxwell had gone.

"And quite near Pierrot," said Anne, with a smile.

Georgie nodded, and then looked at Barbara, who was scowling.

"And near yours too, I suppose?" she asked timidly, because she did not want to make an enemy of this girl.

"Oh, I haven't a pony of my *own*," said Barbara. "It wasn't one of mine I'd come to look at this afternoon, when I saw you with your mouse. *I* haven't got relations able to give me horses!"

Everyone felt uncomfortable, and Georgie most of all. She thought of it now, lying in bed. When one came to think of it, very few people *had* got relations who either could or would hand over a horse in this manner. The funny thing was that she had always imagined Aunt Milly's sister to be rather badly off. She wondered unhappily if her father would have to pay very much for Penelope's upkeep, and if he would mind. He was not poor, by any means, but there were the twins at school as well, and Peter would be going in the summer. . . .

Peter! The thought of him brought a dreadful pang of home-sickness. She longed for her mother and Peter, and the soft fur and elegant whiskers of King Toby, who was worth all the horses in the world. . . . She felt for her handkerchief, but instead of shedding the expected tears, she fell fast asleep—to dream that she was the star turn at a big gymkhana, jumping gloriously on a lovely pony who shared her triumph and joy.

She was awakened by the clamour of a deep-toned bell.

"Prayers are at nine o'clock," Miss Primrose announced, after breakfast, "and after that you will go to your form-rooms. On other week-day mornings, beginning to-morrow, you will rise half-an-hour earlier, and help in the stables from a quarter-past-eight till a quarter-to-nine. There will be games for forms One, Two, and Three this afternoon. The middle school and the seniors will report to the stables at two o'clock."

As they went into the hall for prayers, Georgie saw that Susan was looking very disconsolate.

"I'm a Third! *I've* got to play with the kids, while the rest of you see the horses and probably get some riding. It isn't fair!" she fumed. "Just because I've been to sixteen schools and never learnt anything. . . . Mother told Miss Primrose, and she sent me a test to do—and I couldn't do it—so here I am."

"No talking, please," snapped Miss Kennedy, overtaking them. "You must work harder, Susan, that's all!"

"Lessons aren't hard, really, Susan," whispered Georgie. "I'll help."

"Georgia! Did you hear me say No Talking? You," said Miss Kennedy, "have the distinction of receiving the first order mark in this school. For disobedience."

Rosalie grinned at Brenda, and mouthed "Tradition!" at the discomfited Georgie.

But once lessons began, it was better. Georgie might not have worked at the High School, but she was naturally intelligent and had been taught so much by Peter that she easily held her own, when they were all questioned by Miss Kennedy on a variety of subjects. Miss Kennedy was their form-mistress. Miss Primrose had evidently thought that the Fourth was in greatest need of discipline.

Miss Primrose herself taught classics. Georgie's Latin was well above the standard required, and she had even started to learn Greek, which she would not need at the Grange until she was in the Fifth. She began to enjoy herself. She had a desk between Patience and Judy, which had an excellent view of the drive and the beech trees almost as far as the gate.

Just at the end of the morning, when Miss Briac was finishing an interesting French lesson, Georgie and her immediate neighbours saw an enormous horse-transport van turn into the drive. Judy nudged her excitedly, and even Patience showed signs of restiveness. Pam Pinkerton, craning forward, held up her hand.

"Miss Briac, Georgia's horse has arrived! *May* we go and see the unloading?" she begged.

"Why, yes, it is an event, is it not?" smiled Miss Briac, herself a keen horsewoman. "Let us all go. Georgia, how happy you must be to receive so excellent a surprise!"

Georgia gulped nervously. She felt almost faint. For once she had worked really hard; she had enjoyed her lessons, and also the feeling that here at last was something which she could do as well as the others. And now, that wretched Penelope had come to spoil it all. . . .

The Fourth form, led by Miss Briac, marched to the front door and across to the stable-yard. A few moments later they were joined by girls from other forms, who had also seen the van and begged permission to watch Penelope emerging from it. Susan came up to Georgie.

"Here's one of my lunch biscuits. I saved it for you to give her. Take it quickly," she said: "I've nearly eaten it lots of times, and I might yet!"

Georgie took it gratefully, well aware of the sacrifice. The van had stopped now, and Maxwell and the other grooms were talking to the laughing driver. A boy jumped from the cab and ran to unlock the door.

The Grange held its breath.

Georgie stared at the van, fascinated. In another moment, she thought, the frightful creature of her dreams would come leaping forth with a deafening neigh. She stiffened as a strange sound rent the air. *That* wasn't a neigh! No horse on earth could make that noise. It sounded like—like—

Silent from sheer amazement, they all watched the boy lead a little brown donkey down the plank. Georgie felt physically ill with shock and relief. And then, as Barbara began to titter, she realized that Uncle Archie's sense of humour had made her the laughing-stock of the whole school.

"Miss Kane?" said the driver, looking round with a broad smile. "Note for you."

Georgie held out her hand for it, numbly. Barbara, Brenda, Rosalie, and Laura were laughing loudly, and some of the younger ones were joining in. The little donkey stood there, sad and puzzled. She was old, and her coat was matted and unkempt.

"Why, she's a darling!" Georgie cried, and ran forward. She stroked the long brown ears, and patted the velvety face. Penelope looked up at her, as if asking what it all meant. Susan and Teepoo joined her a moment later, and Maxwell came up to them. Georgie looked at him defiantly: was he laughing too? He was not.

"That's right, miss," he said. "It's a poor rider as won't stick up for his own mount. She's been a good little moke in her time. I call it a shame to make a mock of a dumb animal." And he patted Penelope's head.

"Not so dumb, though," Barbara said perkily, though she had stopped laughing. "Poor old thing. . . . What'll you do with her, Georgia? She's past giving rides at the seaside."

"I shall keep her," said Georgie. "She's mine, Maxwell, could she stand my weight?"

66

Her coat was matted and unkempt.

The laughter broke out afresh. The old groom looked down at her kindly.

"Well, miss, it's like this: maybe she could, but what good would it do? Only spoil you for riding a horse when the time comes."

"The time *won't* come," Georgie answered, swallowing a sob.

"It may and it may not. But I'll lay it will," he said quietly. "You've got the right feeling for animals, and that's half the battle. Like to come along of me and see her go into her box?"

"Reckon she could do with a good feed," said one of the other grooms.

It was true. Penelope was much too thin. She looked as if no one had loved her or bothered about her for a long, long time.

"He's putting her in a box!" whispered Brenda. "Just like a real horse—he must be crazy—"

But old Maxwell had quick ears.

"Horse or not, she be a real animal, Miss Deacon," he said sharply, and led Penelope away.

Anne was one of those who were making a fuss of Penelope. She skipped along beside Georgie and Susan, and called to her sister.

"Do come and watch, Ruth—such fun!"

But it was not fun to Georgie. When Penelope was safely installed in the loose-box, looking ridiculously small but already munching happily at a truss of hay, she wandered out of the stable, blind with tears. Ruth caught her up.

"What's wrong? Are you so disappointed?" she asked. "Don't cry, whatever you do. Don't let the others see."

Georgie found her handkerchief and blew her nose fiercely.

"It's one of my uncle's practical jokes. I'm hating him, and feeling sorry for Penelope, and wishing myself at the bottom of the sea—all at once," she said: "*That's* what's wrong!"

"And quite enough too, to go on with," said Ruth; "but cheer up now. Penelope will be well looked after,

68

and you won't recognize her presently. As for your uncle, everybody's got trying relations, so don't worry about him. And there's no need to wish yourself at the bottom of the sea—there's nothing wrong with you. You'll shake down here soon enough, if you stop thinking about yourself. What does it matter if a few people do laugh at you? It would have mattered if *you* had laughed at that poor little thing coming out of the van. But you didn't. You saw she was frightened and you went up to her."

Incredibly, Georgie began to laugh now.

"It *was* funny, in a way. Perhaps it was the anticlimax they were laughing at, and not me. Though I'd rather they laughed at me than Penelope, who didn't ask to be a donkey. I suppose," she said, "it's true what Maxwell says, about riding a donkey spoiling one for a horse?"

"Well, they're ridden in quite different ways, you see," said Ruth. "I think it's better than not riding at all—but then I'd think anything was. But Penelope couldn't be ridden yet: she's had a hard time of it, apparently. That's why," she added hastily, seeing Georgie's chin quiver again, "it's such a lucky thing she's come to us."

Judy came pelting out to meet them.

"The gong went for dinner hours ago—do come," she said: "I've been sent to fetch you. Is Penelope settling down, Georgia?"

"Oh, yes, thanks," said Georgie airily. "She's having a good feed now. Maxwell and I are going to build her up!"

Ruth shot her an approving glance and followed at a stately, prefectorial pace, while the other two raced indoors.

After dinner Georgie read the note that had accompanied Penelope. As she had expected, it was from Uncle Archie.

DEAR CURLYLOCKS,

What do you think of your Arab Steed? Your Aunt Kate has had her for years. She was useful in the war for pulling a little governess cart, but since then she has been eating her head off in the meadow. She may not be much to look at, but she'll do for you to learn on, won't she?

Your loving old uncle,

ARCHIE.

P.S. I wish I could give you a proper pony, but times are bad.

Times are bad?—they always were, for him. She had heard him use that excuse a hundred times. The truth was, of course, that he was a failure. She suddenly saw him as a pathetic figure, and her anger died away. She asked permission to write him a letter of thanks.

Georgie never forgot how kind Miss Primrose was about Penelope. One might have thought that such an authority on horses might despise a shabby old donkey, but she had got what Maxwell called the right feeling, and when she made her daily inspection of the stables, she never failed to go into the little shed which Penelope soon shared with Pixie, the lame pony. She would discuss with Georgie the amazing improvement which soon showed in the donkey's condition, due to shelter, proper care, and good food.

"When she's really well," she said, "I'm going to ask you to lend her to the gardener sometimes. He's got one of those old-fashioned mowing machines to be drawn by a pony or donkey. I don't suppose you've ever seen them. Penelope will have to wear little goloshes, and she'll thoroughly enjoy it. Maxwell tells me that you helped to groom the other ponies yesterday, after you had finished with Pixie."

Georgie nodded shyly. Two weeks had passed since term began, but she was still shy.

"And Henry says you are a great help in the harness-room," Miss Primrose went on. "What made you offer to work in there?"

"Henry and Harry were both busy, Miss Primrose, and I was playing with Nancy Andrews," Georgie explained. "She's longing to ride again, poor little thing, and I told her that working on the harness was the next best thing. So we did it."

Miss Primrose smiled and sighed at the same time. This girl baffled her. Georgie was terrified of horses, yet she had gone to the rescue that frosty night and had probably saved Firefly's life. She was nervous and self-conscious, but faithful in her undertaking to look after Pixie, the pony, and Nancy, the six-year-old child who had had a serious illness and might not ride again for a year. She was a girl who loved reading and enjoyed her free time, and yet she sacrificed a good deal of it to coach the backward Susan, who was eager to get into the Fourth form.

Matron had told Miss Primrose privately that Georgie came in for a good deal of ill-natured teasing from Barbara and her friends, and the headmistress was sorry to hear that this difficult girl was quite unable to stand up for herself.

"Do you like it here, Georgia?" she asked now.

"Parts of it, Miss Primrose. I love the house," said Georgie eagerly. "The old part is like history, and I like to think of the things that may have happened there. And I like the work—there'll be so much to tell Peter, when the holidays come. And I like Pixie and, of course, Penelope, and the dogs."

The Thurstons had brought a terrier with them, called Bill, and Laura had a Peke. Georgie used to exercise them sometimes when the others were out riding.

"Make friends," said Miss Primrose. "I suppose a head-mistress oughtn't to admit it, but that's the best part of being at school."

Georgie thought about that conversation afterwards. She wanted to make friends. She had become really fond of the madcap Susan, and quiet Patience, and the good-tempered Anne. She liked Teepoo, too, but it was difficult to see much of her. Teepoo was the most serious-minded of all the girls at the Grange. She had come to England to study, and study she would! She was splendid at games; she could run nearly twice as fast as Pam Pinkerton, whose nickname at her old school had been Lightning. Teepoo was splendid on horseback, too, but although she
71

was devoted to her own pony, Spot (a handsome chestnut, without a spot on any part of him!), she had to be almost forced into the saddle. Her one thought was her work. She was intensely grateful to Georgie, who was teaching her to speak English more fluently; but her pre-occupation in her books made real friendship impossible.

Susan, Patience, and Anne liked Georgie, and so did Judy Thurston. They were all friendly, but they were not friends. It was not only that Georgie failed to share their greatest interest, riding, but that she absolutely refused to talk about it. She would not enter the three main blocks to see the horses fed.

"I'm just not keen on them," she would say.

"Well, you might pretend to be, when you know we are," said Susan once. "I want to tell you what happened at the five-bar gate in Randall's Lane, and you won't even listen."

Georgie shrugged. How could she tell these girls that to hear of their exploits made her sick with fear, just as she had been when those dray horses bolted all those years ago?

All the same, as the days went on, she did feel more at home. Brenda and Rosalie were nicer to her now, so she enjoyed herself sometimes in bedroom Eight. She liked her school work, and was learning the piano for the first time. Mr. Simmons, the visiting master, believed she had talent in that direction, and openly rejoiced that she had not had previous lessons but could study his methods from the first.

It was a pity that Barbara Snow was also musical. She *had* learnt before, and Mr. Simmons was making her unlearn a good deal, with the result that at the present time she was reduced to the scales and exercises that Georgie played. One week Georgie was given a simple march to learn, and Barbara still had exercises. She was a petty girl, and she had never liked Georgie. Ruth Conway had spoken to her quite sternly after the Penelope incident, reproaching her for laughing and jeering as she had; and Barbara felt that Georgie was to blame.

One day somebody remarked upon the uncanny likeness the three Thurstons bore to one another. They were all very tall and thin, and their colouring was identical.

"When they're grown up, they'll be known as the Three Tall Thurstons," Pam prophesied.

Georgie, remembering an old rhyme, quoted thoughtlessly: " 'Three Tired Toads Trotting to Tewkesbury.' "

"What's *that* from?" demanded Susan, who was becoming a second Teepoo in her thirst for knowledge. "Shakespeare, isn't it?"

Georgie, explaining gently that it was not, failed to hear Barbara's triumphant snigger. The next day happened to be Sunday, and Judy Thurston had asked Georgie to be her partner on the walk to church. Georgie stood waiting for her, and at last Judy came, her nose in the air.

"I'm walking with Joy," she said briefly.

"But—" began Georgie.

"My sisters and I," said Judy, with unwonted dignity, "don't much care for being called toads behind our backs. That's all."

"But I didn't—I—" Georgie stopped. She had never been good at explaining herself. "All right," she said, "I'll walk by myself."

But she was not allowed to do that. She had to walk through the village with Miss Kennedy, who lectured her all the way because there were holes in her gloves.

CHAPTER SEVEN

HORSE SENSE

THERE was to be no half-term holiday. Georgie could not believe it when Miss Primrose first gave it out. She had been counting on a week-end at home.

"As this is our very first term," said Miss Primrose, "it would be a pity to break the continuity, so to speak. Besides, Easter will be early this year, and we shall have a holiday then, as you will celebrate it at school. There is to be a gymkhana in Randall's Meadow on Easter Monday, and although few of you will be competing in the more spectacular events this year, I propose that we shall all spend the afternoon there, and that certain girls, whose names will be announced later, shall enter for the Trotting, and one or two other events. Dr. and Mrs. Lake have kindly invited us to tea in their garden. We shall have to have it in relays, of course, because of the ponies, but I think we shall have a very happy day."

This was said after prayers one Saturday morning, and as the girls settled down to their mending—for Matron insisted upon this weekly hour of penance—they discussed the forthcoming gymkhana from all angles.

"Trotting!" snorted Barbara. "Why can't we show off our jumping? I bet those Lakes and the other purely riding-school pupils will get a look in. Why don't you ask to enter something, Patience? You're an old riding-schoolite."

"I'm a 'G' now, though," laughed Patience. They had discovered at the village shop, where they bought their sweets, that the local people called them "The G's", because of their hat-bands. G's and Gees made a pleasing pun, and the girls liked their new name.

"Still—*trotting!*" grimaced Barbara. " 'Three Tired Toads Trotting to Tewkesbury', as Georgia would say."

Joy and Judy Thurston looked up from their sewing. June, their eldest sister, was exempt from this Saturday torture. The Sixth could mend their attire when and where they liked.

"Was *that* all Georgia said?" asked Judy. "You didn't say she was quoting, Barbara. You said *she* said—"

"Now, now," said Matron, "no names, no pack drill. Let me see that stocking," she demanded, looking at the red-faced Barbara, who had quite forgotten that the Thurstons were present.

Afterwards, Judy came up to Georgie.

"Sorry," she said bluntly. "I thought you'd said we
74

reminded you of toads. Why on earth didn't you say you'd been quoting something?"

"I couldn't," Georgie muttered. She felt rather heroic, and quite expected that Judy would ask her to shake hands. But Judy only stared at her.

"You're feeble," she said. "That's what's the matter with you. I don't mean you ought to have sneaked on Barbara, but you could have explained a bit. Why can't you be more like other people?"

Georgie winced. That old cry again: "Why can't you be more like Gerry?"

"Why can't they let me be myself?" she thought angrily, and went off to the stables.

Harry and Henry were grooming Mademoiselle. Georgie watched from a safe distance. She loved to see Harry's dexterity with the curry-comb. Henry, who was not so well to-day, was working much more slowly than usual. These two grooms were firm friends. They had been through the war together, in the Remount, and had worked with horses all their lives. Harry was big and bluff and could barely read and write. Henry was slight and quiet and had had a good education. It would be difficult to find two men less alike, and yet their common interest had made this bond between them. There was a story that Harry had saved Henry's life under fire, though neither man would ever speak about those times. Certainly Henry had been badly wounded. There were pieces of shrapnel in one shoulder still, gradually working their way out. When they reached a certain stage he was to go to the Lennet Magna Cottage Hospital, and after that he would become quite well.

This Saturday he looked pale and wan.

"Chuck us the dandy, Henry," said Harry suddenly.

"Right." But Henry found it an effort to move. "Could you reach it, Miss Kane?" he asked. "It's that brush, see, on the shelf."

Georgie was standing in the doorway of Mademoiselle's stable. She had never dared to go inside. Now, not liking to refuse, she entered, and reached for the dandy-brush. In her trepidation she slipped and nearly fell, and Made-

75

moiselle made a startled sound and reared. Georgie saw those waving forelegs, and all but fainted. She did manage to seize the brush, however, and gave it to Harry.

"Thanks, miss. Why, you look all of a twitter! Not used to my lady's tricks, are you? But you've no call to look like a ghostie," said Harry, in surprise. "Didn't you see as I'd got her? You wants to trust people more, that's what."

Mademoiselle made a startled sound and reared.

"Steady on, Harry. Mademoiselle's a bit of a tartar, you know. She's not for novices. I'm sorry you had a scare, Miss Kane," said Henry. "Like to feed her a piece of sugar? When she's in her box again, I mean."

"No, thank you," said Georgie, wondering how anyone dared to feed her at all. "I think I'll go and see the ponies now."

"Why not ask Maxwell if you can give a hand with

Rockie?" asked Henry. "He's gentle as a lamb. You mustn't judge all horses by Mademoiselle here. It's breeding makes her this way—that and a bit of temper. But she's all right in the proper hands. Miss Primrose, now, she looks a treat on her."

"Will she ride her at the gymkhana?" asked Georgie, edging away.

"No. She's not ready yet—our Maddy isn't," said Harry. "She's got to calm down a good bit yet, afore she can be ridden with other horses. Led Henry a proper dance this morning, she did—that's what's made his shoulder play up."

And he showed Georgie where Mademoidselle had kicked the wooden walls.

"Oh dear! Suppose she broke loose?" Georgie shuddered. "I think she ought to live in a concrete stable."

Both men laughed at that.

"Don't worry: this may be only wood, but she'll move into Block C before long. This'll last her all right. It's as strong as a castle," said Henry.

When Georgie was out of earshot, he looked at Harry.

"That's a born rider if ever there was one. Ever noticed how she handles the ponies? And the way she grooms that rum old donkey? It's a downright shame she's a bundle of nerves. That's the sort of girl I'd like to teach," he said. "Sensitive. Good hands. Able to see the horse's point of view."

Harry grunted.

"Plumb scared, she is, and hopin' no one'll spot it. It'd take an earthquake to get her on a horse. But it's a pity. I like the way them juniors calls for 'er the moment something's wrong. There's good stuff in her, only it'll never come out."

The girls were all working in the yard this morning. Some, with long rakes, were engaged in clearing up, others were stacking fresh hay, and those who possessed horses of their own were busily grooming them. When Georgie and her little shadow, Nancy, had finished the small jobs they did for the ponies, they went to the harness-room, only to find Judy, Laura, and Patience working there.

"Can't we groom Penelope, Georgie? Oh, do let's!" Cried Nancy, so eagerly that Georgie was sorry to have to tell her that she had already done this.

"Well, let's go into 'A' and see Rockie," begged Nancy. "It's Pam's turn to do him to-day."

Georgie usually had some excuse ready when the child asked her to go into any of the three main blocks, but she did not like to disappoint Nancy twice.

"All right," she said. "Come on."

Rockie had been given his name because of his likeness to the typical rocking-horse which has graced so many nurseries. He was dappled, with an arched neck, thick flowing mane, and a most benevolent expression. He had a sweet, gentle nature and nerves of iron; he had never been known to show the slightest signs of temper. He had no great speed, but he could stand any amount of work, and was the accepted mount for novices, or those who lacked confidence.

Pam looked up with a smile.

"You're just in time," she said to Georgie and Nancy. "I've promised to saddle Pierrot for Anne, as she's cut her finger. Just finish him off, will you?" and she moved away.

It sounded casual enough, but Georgie suspected it was part of a deep-laid plan. Several of the girls had tried to interest her in the horses, and she was sure that Pam wanted her to have contact with Rockie.

"Goody, goody!" said Nancy, and she seized the dandy-brush. "Georgie, could you hold up his near hind-leg?"

"He—he mightn't like it. He doesn't know me," said poor Georgie.

Immediately there was a burst of laughter from farther down the stable. She had not realized that Barbara and Rosalie were there.

"Quite right, Georgia! Always wait to be introduced!" said Barbara. She came forward, a mocking light in her khaki eyes. "Sir Rockie Dapple Grey—Miss Georgia Jitters. That do?"

Georgie looked away, flushing. Nancy tugged at her hand.

"She's being nasty to you, Georgie! Don't let her. Why don't you say something?" she cried.

"I'm too busy to chatter," said Georgie. "I'll lift his leg if you've got the brush ready."

She did so, setting her teeth. Rockie turned his head and gave her a friendly look.

"He's saying 'Don't tickle!'" the child laughed, and set to work.

Miss Primrose came in, very trim and handsome as usual in her well-cut riding clothes. After talking generally, she said to Georgia, "Shall we go to see Penelope? Tidy up Rockie's things, Nancy, and then help Pam."

Georgie saw that Miss Primrose wanted to speak to her alone, and wondered what was coming now. As they talked to Penelope—now sleek and well and obviously happy—she felt very glad that Miss Primrose had not entered Block A a few minutes earlier, in time to hear Barbara introducing Rockie.

A moment later, however, she realized that Miss Primrose *had* heard.

"Is this the first time you have touched Rockie?"

"Yes, Miss Primrose." Georgie went scarlet.

"But you like him, don't you? Everyone does. I had him from a foal, you know. I was about your age, and living here with my grandparents. I was allowed to break him in. Georgia, my nephew is coming to spend next week-end here. He's bringing Firefly, who's quite fit again now. He will want to thank you."

"He needn't. I mean, he has. And I didn't do much—I didn't *want* to do it at all. I'm afraid he thinks I'm brave," said Georgie, "and I'm not. Couldn't you tell him, please, Miss Primrose?"

"You mean that you don't like sailing under false colours? Quite right. But *are* they false?" asked the head-mistress, smiling. "You have plenty of courage, you know. It cost you far more to go to Firefly's aid than it would have cost any of my other girls. I'm afraid you're not altogether happy here, and I must say that if I had known you disliked horses, I should have advised your mother to send you to another school. You know it is not our
79

wish to force you, and it's purely for your own sake that I speak now. You're frightened, aren't you? Why?"

Georgie stroked Penelope's ears. It was a relief that Miss Primrose knew at last.

"Yes, I am frightened," she said simply. "It isn't that I don't like horses. I pretend I'm not interested, but I am really. It's just that they're so big and strong, and—and you never know when they're going to bolt and pin you against the wall."

Her voice shook. Miss Primrose looked at her keenly.

"Which wall?" she asked.

"Why, the one in London, but I don't remember really—I was only about three," Georgie answered, and then her eyes widened. "How funny! I haven't thought of that properly for years. I don't even remember that nurse's name. . . ."

"What was the horse like?" Miss Primrose asked quietly.

"There were two. Dark grey, I think. Great big ones harnessed to a huge dray. They bolted, you see, and nearly squashed me, and nurse told me not to tell, because she didn't want Mother to know she'd taken me to that street where her friends lived. But it's ages ago," said Georgie.

"I'm glad you've told me. I think we've got to the root of the matter. Look," said Miss Primrose. She rolled up her right sleeve, and showed the girl an ugly scar. "My dog bit me when I was sixteen and was getting his paw out of a trap. I knew he couldn't help it, but it put me off dogs for years, though I love them really. So you see I do understand. But we have to try to forgive and forget. Animals are like people: they do all sorts of unpredictable things when they're frightened or hurt, and sometimes they injure us, just as people do. But we mustn't judge them by that. Horses are, as you say, very big and strong compared with us, but they are completely in our hands. Which do you think would be a worse thing to remember, Georgia, in days to come—being frightened by bolting horses, or the knowledge that you, by harsh treatment, had frightened one yourself?"

80

"Oh, it would be much worse to know I'd frightened one myself," Georgie said at once.

"Yes. But I don't think you ever will. I've often meant to thank you for your help with the ponies. Maxwell says you're very good. Now," Miss Primrose went on briskly, "I must be off—I'm going for a good long gallop with the Lakes and our Sixth form. Do you know, I don't think you'll worry so much about those dray horses now you've told me about them. After all, you can remind yourself that you showed courage even then, as I imagine you kept that promise your nurse had no right to demand."

Georgie began to laugh. Miss Primrose, smiling herself, asked why.

"Well—oh, it sounds awful cheek—but I was just thinking how different you are from what I thought you'd be. I mean—"

"Yes, you hadn't a very flattering opinion of me, had you! Well, when you hear that my nephew has arrived, you needn't feel at all embarrassed. You'll find that he will respect you just as much, and feel just as grateful, even though you have nothing to do with the horses."

Georgie stayed with Penelope for a little while, thinking. She was thankful Miss Primrose had mentioned the nephew's visit. "I'd have got into no end of a flap if I'd heard about it suddenly," she thought. "How decent she is! How decent they all are, with a few exceptions. . . . I wish—oh, I do wish I could learn to ride by magic, and surprise them all one day! If I could enter for that gymkhana on Easter Monday, and go in for the jumping. . . ."

But alas, she had heard Maxwell say several times that there is no royal road to riding—or indeed, to anything else worth doing. She went into the yard, and saw a crowd of girls ready and mounted, waiting for Harry's signal to start for that morning's practice on Randall's Common. On an impulse she went up to Rockie, whom she now regarded as a friend. He turned to look at her, and Rosalie, who was riding him, jerked his head back. He started. His hooves clattered a little on the ground. Instantly Georgie shrank back.

"Here piece of sugar," said Teepoo, who was also mounted. "Come give it to Spot."

She held it out to Georgie. Spot looked round expectantly.

"Sorry, I'm in a hurry," Georgie answered, and walked away.

CHAPTER EIGHT

AN EXEAT

ON Sunday afternoons parents and grown-up friends were allowed to visit the girls at the Grange, and when six weeks of that long and difficult term had passed, Georgie wrote to her mother, asking her to come over by car and bring Peter. Mrs. Kane replied that this was impossible, as the car was now at the garage awaiting the arrival of a new back axle.

And there is another arrival to take place shortly! Daddy will soon be home. He intended to come back in May, but weather conditions are such that he is taking his furlough a little earlier. His letters are full of praise of N'wambo, by the way, and he is so glad you have met Teepoo. Would you like to ask her to stay with us, darling? The Lads will be away for the last two weeks of the holidays, so perhaps that would be a good time to choose. Or, if you don't want Teepoo, invite any other girl you like. What a lovely school it must be!

Georgie folded up the letter with a sigh. She had not really expected her mother to come, because she remembered how nobody visited the twins during their first term at St. John's, for fear of unsettling them. She was in the garden at the time, sitting on the low stone wall near one of the lions. It was early March now, and the trees were in bud, and the ancient lawns were like soft green moss. Yes, she thought, it *was* a lovely school. She had described it in minutest detail in her letters home, principally to avoid writing much about the girls.

Most of them were still quite friendly towards her, and she was happier than she had expected to be; but she felt very much of an outsider, except when she was with little Nancy and her friends, who were always trying to persuade her to play their weird and exhausting games. John Primrose had arrived for the promised week-end, and —thanks to Miss Primrose's tact—Georgie had met him without the slightest embarrassment. Hc had asked if he might take her out to tea, but Miss Primrose refused, knowing that the other girls would be curious and ask questions about Firefly which Georgie would not care to answer. So he had bought her an armful of books instead —beautifully illustrated books about horses, which she treasured, and studied sometimes.

She heard the bell ring, and went slowly back to her form-room. On the way she passed Teepoo, and, remembering her mother's letter, stopped and spoke to her.

"My father will be home soon—perhaps in the holidays. Will you come and stay with us, Teepoo? You could bring Spot—there's a nice field behind our garden."

Teepoo beamed. Her whole face became one huge smile.

"I like to see Kane family—"

" 'I *should* like to see *the* Kane family.' Will you come, then?" asked Georgie, feeling quite excited. She had never issued an invitation on her own before.

"For a week-end—may I? No bring Spot. I mean, I will not bring him. I stay all holidays in London, you know with lady who bring me to England. She doctor— she teach me much. But I like to come to your home for one night, and see your mother, brothers, cat, and friend of my father."

"All right, then. That's fixed," Georgie said, and was aware that Susan was beside her.

"I've been sent out in disgrace!" said Susan, trying to look subdued. "Judy gave me some little apples to give Aggie just as we were coming in from break, and I only

83

ate one—well, nearly two. . . . And Miss Kennedy saw, and sent me out. It was Lit., you know. We'd just come to, 'If music be the food of love, play on', and she says I've got to stay in this afternoon and write out 'If apples be the food of horses, do not eat them' fifty times."

Then, as Teepóo moved away, she looked curiously at Georgie.

"You haven't asked *her* to stay with you, have you?"

"Yes, I have. Why not? You were the first to say that she was just like the rest of us," said Georgie.

"Oh, I don't mean that—I'd say the same if she were pink or blue or tartan! I mean—the waste," said Susan. "Teepoo just wants to work—she's said so lots of times: she wants to go and see horrid skeletons and things in museums. And yet you ask her to stay at your home in Devon, with all those gorgeous moors and streams—you don't think of someone like poor old Patience, for instance, who has such a deadly time at home, though she never says so. Or Pam, who has to live in London and loves the country. Or even—" She paused for breath. "I was going to say *me*, only I take it back. I eat too much!"

Georgie looked dazed, as well she might, but before she could answer, the door of her form-room opened and Miss Waite peered out.

"Georgia? Come in at once, please. As you apparently understand the theorem of Pythagoras too well to need my comments upon it, perhaps you will kindly draw the complete figure on the board and explain it, step by step."

Both knew that this was beyond Georgie's powers. A painful ten minutes followed, after which Georgie was allowed to go to her desk on the understanding that she resumed her attack on the hated theorem that afternoon.

"Poor thing—now you won't be able to come out on the common and see Maxwell jumping Mademoiselle over the stream," said Patience, when geometry came to an end.

"She'd rather do a cosy little theorem, though, wouldn't you, Georgia?" Barbara put in. "Mademoiselle might run amok."

"Oh, do shut up!" said Patience, and they all gasped. No one had heard her utter a slang phrase before. She

84

realized this herself. "I must be careful," she murmured. "Guardie would be so perturbed if I said such a thing at home."

Georgie had seen her guardian once—an old, old man who came to the school to visit Patience in an antique "victoria" driven by a whiskered coachman. She remembered what Susan had said.

"Patience," she said in a low voice, "will you come and stay with us next holidays?"

. . . in an antique "victoria".

Patience's round, fair face became absolutely crimson.

"You don't mean it! Me? At your home?" Her eyes shone. "Oh, but Guardie would never let me," she said flatly. "He doesn't approve of new-fangled ways."

The entrance of Miss Briac stopped their conversation, but they resumed it as they washed their hands for dinner.

Georgie was touched by the other girl's patent delight at being asked to stay at Wychwood.

"We're not new-fangled, Patience, honestly—though I don't know quite what it means," she said.

"He'd think you were. He doesn't like—well, slang, or cinemas, or girls in breeches. He made me promise I'd always ride side-saddle if he let me come here. And he said I was never to bring any shrieking hoydens home," said Patience. "Of course," she added hastily, seeing Georgie's face, "I know you don't shriek, and you're not a hoyden—"

"And I don't wear breeches except for stable-chores, when its' compulsory," said Georgie. Many of the girls preferred jodhpurs when they went out, but ordinary cord breeches were supplied as uniform, and worn when there was stable-work to be done.

"And you're quiet, and behave well at table, and don't interrupt people," Patience went on thoughtfully.

"Look here, are you writing me a character, or what?" asked Georgie, in natural wrath.

"No, I was thinking that we'd better arrange for you to come home with me to tea one Sunday afternoon. Then Guardie can see you're not a hoyden, and perhaps he'll let me come to stay," Patience explained.

Thus it was that about ten days later the two girls were fetched by the ancient victoria, and taken to the dismal old house at Lennet Magna where Patience's guardian lived. It was a Saturday, not a Sunday—Miss Primrose let the girls receive visitors on Sundays, but preferred them not to go out—and Georgie was wishing that she had not got to go. This was the afternoon when the girls who were entering for the Trotting event at the forthcoming gymkhana were going up to Randall's Meadow for their final practice, and to her own surprise she really wanted to see how they got on. She could have walked there with Nancy and Miss Giles, the kindergarten mistress, who also did not ride, and it was such a lovely fresh afternoon—much too good to waste on a sour old man who thought everything new-fangled. . . .

She had been working hard when Patience told her it

was time to get ready. Pixie was well again now, and she had actually saddled him all by herself, ready for one of the juniors, and Maxwell had said that he couldn't have done it better himself—

She suddenly turned deathly white, and clutched Patience's hand.

"We must go back!" she said hoarsely.

"We can't—we're nearly there. What *is* the matter?" cried Patience.

"When I came in to get ready," said Georgie, in hollow tones, "I slipped on my coat right away to see if the hole showed too badly—the one I tore when I was throwing sticks for Bill—and I didn't take it off again. I didn't put my dress on. I'm still in my breeches!"

"Oh, *no!*"

"Oh, yes! Look here, Patience, I must go back, or not come at all—"

"No," said Patience, with the calm of despair: "Guardie can't bear people who break appointments and don't keep their word."

"What will he say?" gasped Georgie.

"Nothing. He'll only think!"

The gloomy house stood in a thicket of tall evergreens. The front door was opened by a bent old crone.

"Come in, Miss Patience. Wipe your feet. Will you take a chair in here till the master's ready?"

She ushered them into a cold, damp room that smelt of mothballs.

"She's a dear really," Patience whispered. "But you see she sees so few strangers. Keep your coat buttoned as long as you can."

Soon the old dame took them to another room, larger and full of relics of more spacious days.

"This is Georgie Kane, Guardie."

"Georgie? A boy's name," said the patriarchal figure which had risen at their entry. Georgie looked up at shrewd dark eyes in a forest of bristling white eyebrows.

"My name is Georgia really, sir. I was called after my great-grandmother, who is Georgina."

" 'Is'?" he repeated. "Not 'was'? You have a great-grandmother living? Good!—I like to hear of old stock wearing well."

"She has a great-grandfather too, Guardie," said Patience.

Of course he was delighted. He was really rather a dear old man, once one grew used to his skull-cap and those truly formidable eyebrows. He said several times that old things were best, and looked round the room with satisfaction.

"Nothing new-fangled in here, thank you! Prettyboy is the one exception—eh, Patience?"

Prettyboy was the canary, who lived by the window in an ornamental gilt cage. The old man rang for tea, and when it came, brought forward a chair for Patience and gave her a little bow.

"My châtelaine," he said to Georgie. "Pray, will you not remove your coat?"

"No, thank you!" she said emphatically, accepting a cup and saucer of such fragile porcelain that the least pressure would have smashed it.

Patience looked demure—and somehow very pathetic, when one considered that this stuffy room was her usual environment. She was wearing one of the old-fashioned dresses her guardian had chosen for her, of thick navy serge, with a long and rather tight skirt.

"Yes, Prettyboy is our only concession to youth," he rambled on, speaking as if Patience and Georgie were the same age as himself. "I must have his cage mended. A mouse ran up the curtain yesterday and entered my Prettyboy's domain. Canaries can die of fright. . . . Listen to his beautiful song: compare it with the deafening cachinnations which are termed music nowadays!" He was well away now. He let his tea grow cold as he rambled on. "Progress! *Faugh!* Monstrous vehicles ruining the roads, uncouth hoydens in breeches passing themselves off as their brothers—I am glad you agree with me," he added more calmly, looking at Georgie, who had made a small sound of sheer amazement.

"I—" Suddenly she felt an utter hypocrite. "I'm afraid I don't, sir!" she said, and took off her coat. "We've got a car, and I love the wireless; and if I did ride, it wouldn't be side-saddle—though everyone says Patience looks awfully nice in her get-up—"

"Oh!" cried Patience, at this point. "There's a mouse in the cage again!"

The canary was too frightened to make a noise. It stood there fluttering, while the mouse darted to and fro. Patience ran to the rescue, but the cage was high, and her long skirt got in the way when she tried to climb on a chair. Georgie pushed past her, and with one leap gained the arm of an antique sofa, just below the cage. She reached up, and the mouse escaped.

There was a silence. Prettyboy gave a faint twitter.

"As you are in that position," said the old man, "perhaps you will be kind enough to lower the cage. You will see a pulley. I thank you, Miss Georgie. My coachman shall attend to it immediately. He is a most useful young fellow—most useful." (He was long past sixty, by the way.) "And now, if you will both be seated again, I will ring for fresh tea," he said grandly.

"Oh, no, Guardie, please don't," said Patience, who felt that she could not bear much more. "I think we ought to be going back. I will fill up the hole in Pretty's cage until Albert comes to mend it."

"Very well, my dear child. Punctuality is a most estimable thing. I have enjoyed your visit, short though it has been."

Georgie looked at Patience. "Ask him!" she signalled urgently. But Patience shook her head.

"If you please," said Georgie, taking the bull by the horns, with the air of one expecting to be tossed, "we really came—at least, I did—to see if you—if you please, I am *not* a hoyden!"

"Certainly not!" he said warmly.

"And we'd take great care of her," Georgie rushed on, "and not teach her slang, or let her wear—what I've got on now! So if—"

"Patience," he said, in some alarm, "I fear your friend is suffering from some temporary disorder of the brain."

"No, Guardie. She's just trying to tell you that she wants
89

me to stay with her next holidays. But of course," said Patience quickly, "she knows that I cannot go."

"And why not, pray? I assume that her parents will communicate with me?"

Georgie assured him that they were most punctilious about such things, and he nodded slowly.

"In that case, my dear Patience, I think the change of air will benefit you, and I am glad that you have made a friend who is both resourceful and *honest*."

An as he emphasized the last word, he glanced with something like amusement at the offending garments.

"But for certain modern ideas," he added, "Prettyboy might have been slain by that intruder. Well for him that you came to-day!"

"Well for us, too!" laughed the girls, as the victoria took them back to the Grange.

CHAPTER NINE

DRY BONES

THAT little incident did Georgie good, and cemented her friendship with Patience, who was openly delighted at the prospect of visiting what she called a "real" family. The story of Prettyboy's narrow escape—which Patience told in a way that could throw no ridicule on her guardian—amused the girls, and showed them that the timid Georgie did at least possess presence of mind.

"I'm most *awfully* glad you can have Patience," Susan told Georgie more than once. Her face looked rather solemn, however, and at last Georgie asked her why.

"You didn't mean it, surely, when you said I might have asked *you?*" she hazarded, and Susan looked away. They were in the cloakroom at the time, washing paint off their hands after an art class.

"I wasn't *hinting*," said Susan loftily. "After you with the pumice. Oh, I might have come if you'd coaxed me!"

"Where *are* you spending the holidays, Sue?"

"With Uncle James," was the lugubrious answer. "He's a professor, so he thinks other people are all ig-igger—that word I can never say. Just because one doesn't see the use of history! Of course he's not altogether bad," said Susan, trying to be just. "He did give me Black Aggie, and he's often had me to stay when my people have gone to places where I'd be in the way. They're off to the Hebrides this spring, and I'm too bad a sailor to face that."

"Come to us at the same time as Patience, then," said Georgie. "I'll have to ask Mother, but I know there'll be room, because the twins will be away."

"Oh, Georgie!" Susan leapt for joy. "I *will* try not to eat so much!"

"Mother'll *want* you to eat. We live in the country, remember—you can eat all day if you like," laughed Georgie, who had grown to like Susan very much.

Tea awaited them, and then two solid hours of preparation. As there were only thirty of them at present, they all did their preparation together in the Fourth-form room, which was one of the largest rooms in the house. This evening it was Miss Briac's turn to be in charge, and one of the maids came in to speak to her.

"A parcel has come up by carrier for Miss Teepoo," she said. "Miss Primrose says, may she come and open it, as it's so heavy?"

Teepoo was already standing up, her face bright with pleasure. Miss Briac nodded, and Teepoo went out with the maid.

"I hope it's tuck!" whispered Susan.

"Susan, '*j'ai mangé*' does not mean 'I have mange'!" Miss Briac exclaimed at the same moment, looking up from the exercises she was correcting. "I must ask you to look up the verb '*manger*', 'to eat', immediately, and learn it by heart."

She was not really cross they could see. In fact, she was trying not to laugh, but for once Susan's face was clouded, and in the bedroom that night, when she and Georgie happened to be alone for a few minutes, she admitted that she was worried.

"If I go on like this, I'll be an—iggeramus all my life," she said dolefully. "I'll never get into the Fourth. I'll still be in the Third when kids like Nancy Andrews get moved up. I wish you could help me, Georgie."

"But I do try to—"

"Oh, I know! I'm frightfully grateful, too. It's my own fault—I don't listen half the time when you do tell me things. I'm *awful*," groaned Susan, in despair.

"Don't be silly!—of course you'll move up to the Fourth in time. Look here, there's one thing I could do," said Georgie, struck by a sudden idea: "I believe I could make you interested in history, anyway, by just exploring this house. We will, the next rainy day."

Susan cheered up at once.

"I like exploring. I think I'll just go and say good-night to Teepoo," she said.

"You know you only want to find out about her parcel," said Georgie, trying to look severe.

Brenda and Rosalie had come back by now, and smiled when Susan came back with the news that Teepoo had not so much as mentioned her parcel.

"I bet she doesn't mean to share it. She'll wait till lights out, and then start munching," said Rosalie.

"You know quite well that Teepoo's not like that," said Georgie, turning white. It was still an effort for her to speak out like this, and the others knew it.

"Oh, I forgot!" Rosalie clapped her hand to her mouth in mock embarrassment. "Your father and hers are buddies!"

Now Georgie was very glad that her father was so friendly with N'wambo, for she liked Teepoo, and looked forward to hearing many exciting tales later on. But she saw that Rosalie meant to be offensive, so she answered coldly:

"You seem to take a great interest in my family."

Susan gave her an admiring glance, but Rosalie was furious.

92

"I'm not taking any cheek from you, Georgie Kane, and you needn't think it!" she said rudely. "Everyone knows what a coward you are. You daren't even take this away from me—"

With a sudden movement she snatched Georgie's blouse, which was—for once—neatly folded on her chair. She threw it across the room to Brenda, who caught it with one hand. It had been clean that morning, and now it would be crumpled. Matron and Miss Kennedy would both remark upon that fact next day.

Georgie hesitated, and then saw Susan going to rescue the hapless garment. She realized that this was *her* battle, and she must fight it. She rushed at Brenda, who lost her balance and slipped.

"Look *out!*" shouted Rosalie.

But she was too late. Brenda had clutched at the cubicle curtains for support, and had brought them down, rods and all. . . .

"What," inquired an icy voice in the doorway, "is the meaning of this disgraceful noise?" And there was Miss Kennedy of all people, with Matron close behind her, surveying the angry girls and general havoc.

"Well?" said Miss Kennedy.

"I picked up Georgia's blouse, and she wanted it back, Miss Kennedy," Rosalie answered in angelic tones.

It was true, but, as Susan said later, not true enough. However, there was nothing that Georgie or Susan could say.

"Three of you girls are in my form, and I do *not* expect such noisy, undisciplined behaviour," said Miss Kennedy. "However, this is a house offence, and I will leave Matron to decide upon your punishment."

She walked away, and Matron looked at them sorrowfully. When they were in their bedrooms they were in her charge, and she did not like punishing people.

"You must stay in to-morrow afternoon," she said. "Explain to your mistresses what has occurred, and say that I shall provide you with sewing."

They "groaned with their eyes," as Georgie expressed

it in her next letter to Peter, but said nothing. In silence they climbed into bed.

The three Fourth-formers had to miss hockey, and Susan was forced to forego a ride, as it was the juniors' day for going out. After lunch the four went to Matron's sitting room and each received a pile of face-flannels to hem, for Matron was interested in an overseas mission which needed such things.

"If you want me," she said, looking at the four downcast faces, "I shall be in the linen-room," and she left them.

"Let's have a race!" said the irrepressible Susan.

"I've pricked my finger already," grumbled Brenda.

"I think Georgie ought to be doing this *alone*," said Rosalie, sewing viciously. "If she hadn't been rude to me, I shouldn't have touched her rotten blouse!"

"You were rude first," Susan countered hotly.

"Oh, of course, you would have to stick up for her as you're going home with her!" sneered Rosalie, an unpleasant gleam in her light eyes.

"Oh, let's stop all this wrangling!" said Brenda. "I'm sick of it. I've done two face-flannels. Let's finish them and get away before Matron comes back—we can always say we didn't know she meant us to stay here."

"But she does mean us to stay—" began Susan.

"Don't start *again*," said Rosalie. "Let's have a race, as you said at first."

So they did, and Brenda won, with Susan a close second. Georgie was last, even though her stitches were twice as big as the others'. They sat and looked at each other.

"Oh, well, I suppose we'd better find Matron," said Rosalie, and they went off to the linen-room, which was on the same landing.

It was empty, however. Matron had evidently been called down to the kitchen regions.

"Georgie," said Susan, with a sudden inspiration, "why not explore the house now? After all, we were told we'd got to stay in—nobody said we had to be cooped up in Matron's room. Come on—you *said* you'd teach me history."

It was such a rambling old house that there were many parts of it that the girls had not yet seen. The attics, for instance, were not out of bounds, but they were used as lumber-rooms now, and no one had ever thought of visiting them or had time to do so.

Georgie's eyes brightened. This seemed a good chance.

"All right," she agreed, hoping that Brenda and Rosalie would not come too. But they were bored and wanted to keep out of Matron's way, so they followed when she and Susan made for the funny, narrow little staircase that led to the attics.

There were tiny windows in the staircase wall—mere slits, through which the people who had lived here long ago had watched the approach of enemies and the departure of friends.

"See that hill over there, Sue? It's quite possible that people used to light a beacon on it when anything special happened, such as a great victory. That's how they used to spread news in days before there were daily papers—"

"No newspapers?" Susan asked in horror. "What *did* they wrap their fish in, then? And if they just had beacons, they'd never know if there'd been a victory or a defeat."

"Oh, yes, they did," said Georgie. "Peter told me about it once. There were different kinds of beacon—a sort of code. That's how the news of Waterloo was spread—"

"The station, you know, Susan!" giggled Rosalie.

"I'm not as green as all *that*," said Susan, in a lofty tone. "I know there was a battle of the same name. Go on, Georgie, this is wizard—I can almost see the people hanging out of these windows, waiting for the beacon. . . ."

"Well, they'd have to be cardboard people if they could hang out of these slits," said Georgie. "They're like castle windows—they were made like this so that enemy archers couldn't shoot the defenders of the house. Now we're at the top of the stairs. Isn't it dark!"

"*Brrr!* Ghosts!" jeered Brenda. "Like me to hold your hand, Georgie? Or is it only horses you're scared of?"

"Mee-up!" said Susan. "That's the short for 'miaou

and shut up," in case you don't know. I say, what's that *frightful* noise?"

They stood silent on the dark landing, listening to a strange gurgling sound.

"It's like a witch's cauldron bubbling— Oh, I know! It's the cistern!" laughed Georgie. "It must be in one of these rooms. This house wouldn't have water laid on when it was built."

"No baths? Just that awful ox-in-a-teacup business, in a bedroom?" squeaked Susan. "We had to do that once in a cottage, but I thought there was always hot water laid on in big houses."

It occurred to Georgie that she was teaching Susan history in a very unromantic way, but at least she had succeeded in interesting her.

"Let's see what's in this next room," she said, passing the cistern and trying the next door.

It opened easily, and they went into a large square attic, beautifully panelled in oak. The window was small, and as it was a dull day the room was full of dark shadows. The four girls looked round them with great interest. In one corner was a pile of trunks.

"I bet they're full of old coins and family jewels!" breathed Susan, now quite carried away.

"Hardly," said Brenda, peering at them in the gloom. "They've got Miss Primrose's initials on them, and ordinary luggage labels. This is only a box-room, my child!"

"Still, there might be a secret panel in the walls," said Georgie, seeing Susan's face fall. "Let's tap them now we're here. I've never done this before, but the wood sounds hollow if there *is* a recess."

They tapped for a few minutes, but nothing happened. The oak had been carved in all sorts of fantastic designs of flowers and fruit and animals.

"There's a dear little lion here," said Susan, "with a collar with a real ring in it. Shall I pull it?"

She did so, and part of the panelling about five feet square began to move.

All the girls fairly shrieked with excitement. Susan was quite pale.

A skeleton was standing in the aperture.

97

"I daren't open it! Nobody's touched it for hundreds of years, and—"

"Here, let me come!" said Rosalie, pushing her roughly aside. She tugged at the door, which was rather stiff, and suddenly uttered a scream.

"Oh, it's horrible! Let me get away," she babbled, stepping back on Brenda's toes.

Brenda screamed too, and Susan gave a choking gasp. Georgie was too amazed to make a sound. A skeleton was standing in the aperture, only a few inches from their horrified faces.

Rosalie had rushed to the door, and was tugging the handle.

"I can't open it! It's locked! We're locked in—with that thing! Help, help!" she shouted.

"Let m—me try!" said Brenda, with chattering teeth; but she too was powerless to open the door.

"Listen," said Georgie. She was trembling, but had managed to keep her head. "We'll be all right—they'll hear us in time and let us out. And that skeleton can't hurt us—Oh, Susan!"

That was a cry of consternation, because the red-headed and usually intrepid Susan had dissolved into tears.

"She's frightened to death, and no wonder! It's all your fault!" Brenda said to Georgie.

"It isn't! And I'm not frightened. I'm only so sorry for the poor skeleton," Susan explained, as she fumbled for her handkerchief. "He must have been a Cavalier, and the Roundheads were after him, and he hid, and starved to death—and Mummy's sending me a tuck-box next week!"

"Fat lot of good, your being sorry for the skeleton! Ten to one, *you'll* never see that tuck-box either!" said Brenda. "Let's all yell—"

"No need for that," said Georgie, weak with relief. "I can hear someone coming up the stairs."

Sure enough, approaching footsteps could be heard, and a familiar voice calling anxiously, "Girls, where are you?"

"Matron!" they shouted. "We're here! Locked in!"

An instant later she had opened the door, and was confronting them.

"There is no rule, I know forbidding you to enter Miss Primrose's private rooms, but I should have thought your own common sense— Still," said Matron, "I suppose Teepoo told you that her skeleton was here?"

"Teepoo's skeleton? Then he's not a Cavalier?" Susan burst out.

"What *do* you mean? Did you come upon it accidentally then?" Matron was beginning to understand the tense attitude of the four girls. "It arrived last night, in a box," she said. "A cousin of hers is a medical student, and you know how eager Teepoo is to get on with her studies. It seems that he was able to get hold of this set of bones, and sent it to her for a present. Miss Primrose allowed her to assemble it—the bones are all wired, for demonstration purposes—and then, as it's not a thing we care to have about, we helped her to hang it in this cupboard."

"Then it's not a secret panel," Georgie said, in acute disappointment.

"Good gracious, no! This used to be a maid's bedroom, and she hung her clothes in it, so Miss Primrose says. And you were not locked in, you silly children—the catch of this door needs repairing, that's all. Come down at once," said Matron: "it's nearly time for tea."

They followed her, smarting under the epithet of "silly children", but feeling it well deserved. . . .

"But I do know now that history's real," Susan whispered to Georgie, who felt that the experience had not been in vain.

At tea, however, she heard Rosalie and Brenda holding forth about it at their table, and it was very hard to sit still and listen to the laughter of the other girls.

"—and when we tried to get out, we couldn't," Rosalie was saying: "the door had stuck. Poor old Georgie was as white as a ghost—she thought we were there for life, and actually mumbled something about the skeleton not hurting us! But we all know what she is—"

Susan, engrossed in her tea, did not hear. But Georgie

felt miserably that once again, and this time most unfairly, she had been branded as a coward. Then she looked up and met Teepoo's dark gaze.

"I not there," said the black girl, in her warm, slow voice, "but I know it was not like that."

"Are you talking about your skelly?" asked Susan cheerfully. "He was rather sweet really. I'm so glad he's a modern one, though." She helped herself absent-mindedly to the last cake. "Now I know," she said, "what the Kenpot means by 'the dry bones of history'. . . ."

CHAPTER TEN

MY KINGDOM FOR—PENELOPE!

AS the weeks went by, all the girls began to see the wisdom of having no half-term holiday. The school had taken shape in an amazing way. Everyone knew the rules now, and accepted the daily routine of work and handicrafts, games and riding. On Mondays, Wednesdays, Fridays, and Saturdays, the horses belonged exclusively to the "G" girls. On Sundays they did not go out, except for gentle exercise by the grooms if necessary. On Tuesdays and Thursdays Miss Primrose rode with her outside pupils, while hockey and netball were played at the school.

To fit in so much, and still allow time for music, art, and various hobbies, meant a very carefully arranged time-table. It also meant that the days, packed with so much incident, passed with astounding speed. Even Georgie could hardly believe it when she looked at her calendar one day and saw that there were only three weeks left of this term.

"A week-to-day will be Easter Monday," said Patience, "and Lennet Fair again."

"Lennet Fair? Is that what they call the gymkhana?" asked Susan, perched on the common-room window-sill. It was after lunch, and the girls had changed into riding-kit. She was wistfully watching the stable yard. The Fifth and Sixth were saddling the horses to-day.

"Oh, no, it's nothing to do with the gymkhana," Patience answered. "That's quite a new thing. Lennet Fair has been going on for centuries. I've never been, of course—Guardie says it's very rough—but I used to watch the people going to it, and see the fireworks they always have."

"Are you telling them about the fair, Patience?" asked Miss Primrose, coming in at that moment. Everyone jumped up, except Susan, who had to jump *down* with a guilty thump—girls were not encouraged to sit on the lovely old window-sills.

"It's a very old festival in this region," the head-mistress continued, choosing not to see Susan's lapse. "It's nothing to do with Easter: it's always celebrated at the end of March. In Saxon times, you know, the month of March was called 'Lennet-monath'—which is where we get our word Lent from—and antiquarians think that High Lennet and Lennet Magna were originally settlements made here in this month. Perhaps the fair is to perpetuate that—no one knows now. But for the last few years it has been a very crude affair with none of the old charm I remember, and so I want to ask you all that if any undesirable people should overflow into Randall's Meadow next Monday, not to encourage them or let them touch the horses. Not that I think they will," she concluded, "for the fair is always held at the Beacon, quite two miles farther on. But in order to get there, people from these villages must walk up Randall's Lane."

The girls promised, of course, and then Maxwell signalled from the yard that he was ready for them. The riders went off in haste, and Georgie joined the juniors, who were going for a nature walk. Teepoo went, too, for she was an enthusiastic collector of specimens. She and Georgie naturally walked together, and Georgie spoke of the gymkhana.

101

"I've never been to one before. You're going in for the Trotting, aren't you?"

"No," said Teepoo. "I not ride. Not even go."

"You're not going to watch? Why on earth not?" And then, seeing her companion's face, Georgie wished she could recall the question.

"I have spoken to Miss Primrose. She agrees with me. There will be many present. I should be conspicuous. I not mind at all," said Teepoo with her cheerful smile. "I work, you see."

Georgie said no more, but she thought a good deal. The next day she went to Miss Primrose and asked her if she might stay with Teepoo.

"It's such lovely weather," she said, for spring had come early, and the whole world looked gay. "It seems so—I mean, she works so hard all the time. The gardeners have put up the net on the hard court, and we could have a singles, perhaps."

"I think it's a very good idea, Georgia," said Miss Primrose, who had no idea that Georgie's interest in horses was beginning to awaken, or that she had been looking forward to the gymkhana. Besides, she was a little concerned about Teepoo, who really was working too hard. "Will you tell Matron that I have given you permission to say?—she will be here as well. You and Teepoo can help her to get tea. All the maids are going to the fair, as they are local girls and have never missed it yet."

That was a very happy Easter for everyone at the Grange. Parcels of chocolate or marzipan eggs kept arriving from self-sacrificing relatives, and on the Sunday the weather was so warm that there was a picnic out of doors. The almond trees were in full bloom, and the beds were massed with daffodils.

"If *only* it keeps like this for to-morrow!" sighed the girls.

But the wind rose during the night, and next morning there were fluffy clouds scurrying across the sky.

"Wind doesn't matter," said Ruth, who, with the two elder Thurstons, was going in for the Open Jumping.

"Perhaps it's a good thing it's cooler. If only the rain keeps off!" She caught sight of Georgie, who was studying the weather as anxiously as the rest. "It'll be chilly watching," she told her kindly. "You'll have to wear your big coat."

"I'm not coming," said Georgie.

"*Not coming?*" yelled her form, for she had not told them of her intention to stay with Teepoo.

"Spectators will be roped off," said Barbara. "You couldn't get hurt."

"It isn't that!" flashed Georgie.

"No? What is it, then?" asked Brenda, and she called Susan. "Sue! Did you know your Jonathan's refused to come?"

Susan gaped at Georgie.

"But I thought you wanted to? You said you wanted to see Aggie in the march past. You said—" In her disappointment, she made an unfortunate remark: "You wouldn't be near the horses, you know."

Georgie turned scarlet. It would be impossible to say that she had chosen to stay with Teepoo without giving the impression that she was being noble. This gibe—for gibe it seemed—from Susan was too much. She stalked into the house.

Even Teepoo did not know yet that Georgie was staying behind. She stood by the front door and watched the gay procession setting off, and Georgie joined her.

"Don't they look wonderful, Teepoo? They seem quite different, somehow. Like swans, when they take to water. Look at Patience—that black habit makes her look like an old-time lady. She ought to have a falcon on her wrist. And the Thurstons! They're not a bit pretty really, but on horseback they look smashing."

"Smashing?" asked Teepoo mechanically, and then started. "But, Georgie, you should not be here."

"Oh, yes, I asked Miss Primrose. I thought you'd play a singles with me. Or is it too windy? Isn't it fun," Georgie said dolefully, "to have the place to ourselves?"

"Matron is here," said the literal Teepoo, "and also

103

Henry. He not well enough to go. He stay in yard instead of Jim."

Jim was the stable-boy who helped the three grooms. Georgie remembered now that he had gone to the gymghana with the rest.

"You stay because of me?" asked Teepoo.

"I wanted to stay. Let's walk round the garden," said Georgie.

The wind was rising all the time. It was hardly worth attempting to play tennis. They walked for quite a long time, looking at the various plants and shrubs, and laughing at the First-form garden, whose sole product seemed to be a line of mysterious spiky weeds. Then, feeling rather cold, they wandered back to the house, passing through the stable yard.

It seemed deserted. They went into the small shed to see Penelope and Pixie, who, with Mademoiselle, were the only animals left at home. Then Georgie remembered a pencil which she had left in the harness-room, and went to fetch it.

Here she had a shock. Henry was lying flat on the old army bunk on which the grooms kept some of their tackle. His eyes were closed, and he was very pale. He did not hear her call his name.

She ran back to Teepoo.

"Henry's fainted, I think. Let's find Matron."

They found her sewing some curtains in her own little room. She put her work away as soon as she saw them, and gave a faint sigh. She might have known that an afternoon of unbroken peace was not for her. But her face changed when Georgie told her about Henry, and she hurried out to see him.

The girls waited till she came out of the harness-room, and she looked at them gravely.

"He's conscious now, but in great pain. It's that shrapnel, of course. He knew this morning that he ought to go to hospital, but didn't want to upset Miss Primrose's plans because of the gymkhana. I'm going to take the school car and drive him down at once. You'll be all right, won't you?"

"Of course we will, Matron. Poor Henry!" said Georgie.

"We have tea ready for you," Teepoo promised.

In a few moments Matron had brought the car round, and the girls helped her to get Henry into it. He was plainly furious with himself for having to give in.

"Maybe you'd ask Miss Primrose if she'd let me know how the young ladies got on," he muttered, his face twisted with pain. "I'd like to have seen Miss Ruth on Pierrot. . . ."

They watched the car go down the drive, and then turned back rather aimlessly. The sight of his agony had shaken them, and the Grange felt very empty now that they really were the only people on the premises. It was quite cheering to hear a group of youths shuffling up Randall's Lane, which ran along one wall of the stable yard.

"On their way to the fair," Georgie said, and smiled as the boys' voices rose in a popular tune. They were evidently excited, and there was some argument in progress.

"*She is my LillEE of LaGOONER*—oh, come on, you chaps: I tell you it's a dud 'un!"

" 'Tisn't, then. You wait and see. Where's the matches? Now—*there!*"

There was a shrill screaming sound, and a rocket soared above the wall and disappeared, amidst shouts of laughter.

"I hope they won't send any more up," Georgie said a little anxiously. "Pixie and Penelope will hate it."

But another rocket did appear, and this time it was a faulty one. It spluttered and fell into the yard. Georgie climbed up a short ladder that was propped against the wall, and addressed the boys with a courage she had not possessed before she came to school.

"I say, please don't light any more fireworks just here. The horses don't like them," she said, thinking how flattered Pixie and Penelope would be if they could hear this description of themselves.

The boys—there were about ten of them—grinned back at her sheepishly.

"Sorry, miss! We'll keep the rest till further on," said the biggest, and they clattered up the lane.

Georgie sprang down from the ladder, quite pleased with herself; but Teepoo called to her in a startled tone: "Straw catch fire—see?"

It was true. The second rocket had fallen on to a heap of discarded straw, and it was burning smartly. Georgie and Teepoo picked up two of the drinking-buckets and rushed to the tap. For some time they worked really hard, and at last the sparks were extinguished. They mopped their faces with their handkerchiefs, and coughed. The air was unpleasantly smoky.

"*Phew!*" said Georgie. "Lucky the stables are built of brick. That was quite near enough. As it is, it's caught the door of 'B' block, and that wheelbarrow's all charred. Teepoo, I think we ought to let Miss Primrose know."

Teepoo nodded violently. "Yes. She must know. Stables smoky now—horses not like smoke. Maybe Dr. Lake let some go in his stables."

"Let's ring her up," said Georgie. "At least, it'll mean ringing the Lakes, but they can get her easily.

They went to the office together, and Georgie found the doctor's number. But now another set-back awaited her. The call was switched through to his partner, in Lennet Magna, who explained that he had taken over Dr. Lake's practice for the afternoon, as the whole Lake family had gone to the gymkhana.

She put down the receiver and looked at Teepoo.

"*Wouldn't* this happen, the one time we're left alone!"

"Not worry, Georgie. We put fire out."

"Well, Matron will be back soon—" Georgie began, and then the telephone rang.

"Is that Georgia? Good—I was afraid you and Teepoo would be in the garden. Well," said Matron's voice, very rapidly, "I shall be delayed, I'm afraid. They are so short-handed here that Sister has asked me to help with Henry. You'll be all right together, I know. Goodb—"

"But, Matron—" Georgie began, but it was too late. The line was dead.

"Perhaps the fire wasn't as bad as we thought, Teepoo,"

she said. "We don't want to be told we made a fuss about nothing. Let's go out and see."

But when they returned to the yard, they were appalled at the damage they saw. Most of the smoke had cleared now, and they could see how badly the door had been burnt.

"It doesn't even stay shut," said Georgia. "We'll *have* to let them know, and soon—or the horses'll all come

They set off at a very good pace.

trooping back. Oh, I wish they'd left one—just *one*—behind! Then you could have gone to tell Miss Primrose."

"Yes. I do not mind people staring now," said Teepoo, always ready to put her own feelings aside when there was real need. "Pixie! I ride him."

"But you can't—he's lame again! Didn't you know? Yes, that's why he's been left behind. Oh, it's nothing much—just one of the clinches in his off-forefoot got wrenched a bit, and he's going to the blacksmith's tomorrow. Of course there's Penelope," said Georgie, "but you're too tall."

A sudden shower of sparks made them both jump. The fire was *not* quite out, after all. They fetched more water, and soused the hay again.

"I take Penelope," said Teepoo.

"You will?" cried Georgie, tremendously excited at the thought of her pet's going to fetch aid.

Teepoo laughed. Running in her lithe fashion, she went to Penelope's shed and unfastened her. She led her by her forelock into the yard, and Penelope, who had made several journeys about the grounds, came quite willingly.

"Oh, Teepoo, but she goes so slowly!" said Georgie.

"Not now. You watch," said Teepoo. She pulled off her shoes and stockings, and mounted the surprised donkey, sitting well back towards the croup. Then she dug Penelope's brown sides with her bare heels, and to Georgie's amazement they set off at a very good pace indeed. They were almost galloping before they reached the gates.

Left alone, Georgie sat down on an inverted bucket, and rested her chin on her hands.

"Everyone's useful except me," she thought. "Even Penelope, whom they laughed at when she came. I'm left behind—like the little lame boy who was the only one the Pied Piper didn't take to the enchanted mountain. . . ."

She felt so sorry for herself at that moment that she failed to observe what was happening a few yards away.

CHAPTER ELEVEN

THE FIRST TRADITION

GEORGIE raised her head and sniffed. Yes, the fire had undoubtedly broken out again. She sprang up and ran to the heap of straw, now a blackened bonfire, and looked for more tell-tale sparks. There were none. She seized a rake and stirred it, but although it was still smoking faintly, there was no trace of fire there now.

But the ominous smell persisted. She could not understand it. Suddenly she heard a little crackle behind her, and spun round swiftly. A cry of terror rose to her lips when she saw that the roof of Mademoiselle's stable was burning.

It was easy enough to see what had happened. One of those sparks had been blown there by the high wind, and had caught the dry wood of which that single stable was built. At present there was only a small togue of flame, but it needed very little imagination to realize how the flame would spread.

Georgie dashed to the gardener's shed, some distance away, knowing that the hose was kept there. But it was locked. That and the bicycle-shed were always kept locked, and she had no idea where the keys could be found.

She ran back to the yard and filled all the buckets she could find, though her hands were trembling so that she could hardly control them. Then she carried the ladder across to Mademoiselle's stable, and climbed up to the roof, bucket in hand.

She poured the water on the flames, and they died at once with an angry hiss. But one of the walls had caught as well, and by the time she had fetched another bucket and dealt with that, the flames were licking the roof once more.

In all her life Georgie had never worked as she worked now. Grimy, panting, half-choked with smoke, she laboured backwards and forwards to the tap, and up and down that ladder until she felt as if her heart would burst. But soon she was forced to admit that the fire had beaten her. The stable was burning, and nothing that she could do would stop it.

She thought of running for help—but the Grange was isolated, and it was too risky to rely on any passer-by. Besides, there was so little time. Soon the whole place would be alight, and—what of Mademoiselle?

"I'll have to get her out myself. It's the only way," she said aloud. Once the idea of entering the stable would have horrified her, and as for loosening Mademoiselle—! But now her one thought was to free the animal, whose little snorts of distress were turning to whinnies of fear.

She grasped the door handle, and turned it. Nothing happened. This door, too, was locked.

She ran to the harness room, where a row of keys hung on hooks. She tried them all, but none fitted. A moment's reflection showed her that Maxwell would have a special place for this key, as Mademoiselle was so valuable as well as dangerous.

Part of the roof fell in. The mare screamed. Georgie sobbed aloud and battered the door with her fists, as though her slight strength could break it down.

"I'm coming, Maddy!" she called out, trying to make her voice like Maxwell's. "Hang on a bit longer, old girl. . . ."

The fire was gaining ground every second. There was no longer any possibility of hunting for that key. She tried the door again, frantically, and this time she thought it gave a little. Then she remembered something. This was a door that opened outward. She had seen it open several times, and must have registered that fact without noticing it.

Therefore no amount of battering on *this* side could

have any effect. The only person who could force the door open was Mademoiselle herself.

"I'll have to get in. I can, through that little window. Lucky I'm thin. . . . I'll let her loose, and she'll charge the door. Horses do when they're terrified. Oh, poor Mademoiselle! If only I'm in time!"

Georgie found that she had been saying all this aloud while she fixed the ladder in position under the small window high up in one wall. The fire had not reached it yet, but the wood was uncomfortably hot. She clambered up somehow, and peered through the window. The stable was full of smoke, but she could see the vast dark shape of the thoroughbred mare, writhing and twisting now in her efforts to rid herself of her head-collar. She was screaming now—a sound that would have shaken Georgie's nerves to pieces at one time, though now it only strengthened her resolve to save her.

Human hands had deprived Mademoiselle of her freedom. Human hands, weak and unskilled though they might be, must give her a chance to save herself.

Georgie wriggled through the window-frame, and dropped heavily on to smouldering straw. She noticed vaguely that her hands here hurting, but there was no time to think of that now. Mastering a great wave of terror, she went up to the box.

"It's all right, Maddy! You'll be free in a minute, and then you've jolly well got to get us both out—" she said, and choked. The smoke in here was intense. It seemed to tighten the skin of her face, so that she thought confusedly of withered apples. Only this morning she had given Pixie and Penelope some tiny shrivelled apples, and had felt quite daring, too. . . .

She stumbled as she felt, with closed eyes for the metal ring to which the rope was attached. Mademoiselle, in a paroxysm of terror, drew back sharply, making it all the more difficult to undo the knot. How thankful Georgie was that she had seen Harry and Henry settle the mare in her box! Otherwise, blinded by smoke and hampered by the trembling of her hands, she would never have known what to do.

Mademoiselle rushed at the door

Mademoiselle reared suddenly, and seemed to blame her for what was happening. She lunged at her, and Georgie dodged, just managing to undo the now slackened knot. Then, as Mademoiselle plunged headlong into the stable, she gave the girl a sharp cow-kick which sent her reeling to the floor.

This was the best thing that could have happened. Georgie was half-stunned, and lay still for some moments, thus avoiding injury from those lashing hooves. And then, just as she had hoped, Mademoiselle rushed at the door, and it cracked—and burst open!

The frantic creature galloped away, and a few seconds later a small, dirty figure came crawling out of the blazing stable.

Teepoo's appearance had caused a sensation at the gym-khana, but Miss Primrose, once she had grasped why she had come, lost no time in deciding what to do. She spoke to Maxwell, and he mounted his horse immediately, having put Harry in charge of the rest. Then he and Miss Primrose, followed by Ruth and the three Thurstons—the most experienced riders amongst the girls—set off for the Grange.

Breaking one of the most rigid of the stable rules, they galloped their horses all the way home, not slackening speed till they were actually in the drive. Miss Primrose and Ruth were leading. They reined in and drew aside as Mademoiselle flashed past them. Then, as they turned the corner of the yard, they saw the fire—and Georgie.

Her clothes were burnt in places. Her hands were badly blistered, and her curly dark hair was singed. One leg was bleeding as a result of that kick. But she was smiling, and on her streaked and blackened face the others saw a look of resolution it had never worn before.

"Good old Penelope!" she said in a hoarse little voice. "So she got there after all."

She was always glad to remember afterwards that she did not faint, though everything became blurred. She was dimly aware that Ruth was leading her into the house, and putting her down on a settee in the drawing room.

"How did you get on?" she faltered.

"Pierrot surpassed himself," Ruth smiled, and covered her gently with a rug. Georgie drew several deep breaths to get the smoke out of her system, and fell asleep.

When she opened her still smarting eyes, she was in bed, and Matron and Dr. Lake were in the room.

"How's Mademoiselle?" she croaked.

"Safe and well," said Matron, "thanks to you. And our girls did splendidly at the gymkhana. Ruth and June both have rosettes, and Ruth's won a cup for jumping. From what people have told me, she must have put up a magnicent show. Maxwell said she was an easy first."

When she next woke up, her hands bandaged and not nearly so painful, Matron had some tea ready for her, and held the cup to her lips.

"Please tell me, Matron," said Georgie, "is everything all right now? Oh, and *how* did they get on with the Trotting?"

"Ruth has a cup. Yes, everything's all right, my dear. Miss Primrose telephoned to the fire-brigade, just to make certain that all danger was over—because that wooden stable burned to the ground very soon after she arrived. All the horses are safe, and some have gone over to Dr. Lake's for the night, till the smoke has cleared away. Penelope is back in her usual place, and very proud of herself too. And Maxwell has gone to fetch Mademoiselle, who galloped right up to the Beacon, it seems, and interrupted the fair!"

Georgie giggled, picturing overturned stalls and scattered cocoanuts.

"She was awfully sensible, you know," she said, sobering. "If she hadn't got the door open—"

"There," said Matron quickly, "don't think about that now. Someone else was awfully sensible it seems. Ah, here's Miss Primrose."

The head-mistress came and sat on the foot of Georgie's bed.

"I want to thank you," she said. "Through a combination of circumcstances that won't occur again—I mean that the Grange will never be left deserted again, as next

114

term our numbers will be so much greater that such a thing would be impossible—through a set of peculiar circumstances, you found yourself in a position of sole responsibility. No one could have behaved more admirably. I'm proud of you. We all are—more proud than we can say."

"But I *couldn't* have just left her there," Georgie muttered, blushing furiously.

"No. I see that you couldn't. That's why I'm proud," said Miss Primrose. "Dr. Lake wants you to stay in bed for three days, till your hands are better and that nasty place on your leg is healed. It was a kick, I suppose?"

"Yes, but she couldn't help it," Georgie said, in quick defence of Mademoiselle. "She was so scared that it was a wonder she didn't *eat* me—"

"They never eat meat!" cried a stentorian voice from the door.

"Susan!" exclaimed Miss Primrose. "Who gave you permission to come up here?"

"I'm sorry, Miss Primrose. I know you said we weren't to disturb Georgie. But I bought some toffee-apples from a man at the gymkhana, and I've saved her one," said Susan, in muted tones, as she held out her sticky offering.

"Come in," said Miss Primrose—quite unnecessarily, as Susan *was* in by this time. "But if we let Georgia stay in this room, you and Brenda and Rosalie must be very quiet."

The doctor had said that as Georgie was a nervous girl, it would be better for her to remain in her own room rather than be moved to the sick bay. Miss Primrose was glad to see that she welcomed Susan.

"I couldn't eat more than half the toffee-apple," Georgie was saying, from the pillow.

"Couldn't you really? Oh, goody! No, I don't mean that," Susan exclaimed in contrition, as she produced a penknife. "Miss Primrose, won't you have a piece?"

"No, thank you. I shall have some tea presently," the head-mistress answered with suitable gravity, as she rose. "Remember, Susan, I rely on you not to make a noise."

"I won't, truly, Miss Primrose. But I *can* just tell her, can't I, how absolutely thrilling it was when Penelope came careering up to us? Oh, Georgie, when Teepoo told us how you said if only there'd been a horse left behind, it reminded me of Julius Cæsar!" cried the irrepressible Susan. "You know—in the Wars of the Roses, wasn't it? When he said 'A horse, a horse—my kingdom for a horse!'"

"But he didn't—and it wasn't—" Georgie was beginning, when Miss Primrose paused in the doorway, and turned round.

"Susan," she said, "I may as well tell you now that next term you will be moved up into the Fourth Form. Not," she added severely, "that Julius Cæsar was ever reported to have made such a wish, nor was he present at the Wars of the Roses—but you have tried very hard, and I think I can trust you to go on trying. You may stay with Georgia for half an hour."

She went away, and the two girls were alone. Susan dropped her usual manner, and became very quiet.

"Does it hurt much, Georgie?"

"My hands sort of prickle. It's not too bad, though. I say, Sue, don't laugh," said Georgie, "but I'm going to start riding next term."

"*What?*"

"Don't yell like that, or they'll turn you out! Yes, I am. I decided just now, when Miss Primrose was talking. I want to—be like other people," Georgie tried to explain. "And I don't think I'll ever be frightened of horses again."

Susan stared, one cheek distended with toffee-apple.

"I should have thought you'd feel worse than ever."

"No. It's funny, but I don't. I was so terrified this afternoon that it kind of worked itself out. Like geometry, you know," said Georgie dreamily. " 'The greater includes the less'—do you see what I mean?"

"No, I don't, but I'm not in the Fourth yet!" Susan munched pensively. "I suppose it's because you felt so sorry for Maddy. You don't feel scared of people when you're sorry for them."

"Yes, partly that, and partly knowing that although

116

she was so big and swift and powerful, I had hands, and she hadn't. And partly," said Georgie, "seeing little Penelope trotting so gamely down the drive. I'd love to ride, Sue. I dreamed once that I was jumping at a gymkhana—"

"Jumping is the most exciting thing on earth," said Susan.

Georgie enjoyed those three days in bed, for she had many visitors, and all the nicest books in the library were brought up for her perusal. By Miss Primrose's orders, no one said very much to her about the fire, but she knew that she had gained a place for herself in the school at last. Even Barbara came to see her. When, on the fourth day, she came downstairs for the first time, she went out to the stables with the other girls for the early morning work, although her hands were still bandaged.

"You can't do much just yet, Miss Kane," said Harry, "but just pop along to see Pixie in his new shoes—he's missed you cruel."

"I've been to him every day, Georgie," said Nancy, hard on her heels, as usual, "but he kept on looking round for you. So did Penelope."

So Georgie went to see her friends, and afterwards let Nancy take her into Blocks A, B and C, where the horses were now back in their usual places. She patted Rockie, knowing that next term she would receive her first lessons in riding from him, and, at Susan's request, went to make friends with Black Agnes. She realized now how gentle and reliable all these animals were, and wondered at her own foolishness in not seeing this long ago. If they had been the savage creatures she had imagined, was it likely that girls would be allowed to groom them unattended? She stroked Spot's muzzle, and Teepoo, brushing mud from his legs, looked up and grinned.

"I have a secret," she said.

"Oh, Teepoo, what?"

"If I tell, no secret. You wait," was the mysterious reply.

"Dash, there's the bell!" said Susan. This was the warning bell that rang ten minutes before the bell for prayers, to allow the girls to tidy up ready for the grooms to carry on.

Georgie, who had no tidying up to do, wandered into the yard and came face to face with Maxwell, who beamed at her.

"Glad to see you up and about, Miss Kane. Want to see Mam'selle in her new box?"

Georgie hesitated for just one instant, and then nodded.

Mademoiselle was in the sick quarters, fortunately not in use at present. She looked round at Georgie with her beautiful but still wild eyes, and gave a few waltzing steps. Maxwell opened his mouth to tell Georgie that she was quite secure, and then saw that the assurance was not needed. Georgie was looking with concern at the patches on Mademoiselle's back.

"She was scorched, then? Poor Maddy, I didn't know. She was wonderful to keep her head as she did, when she was in pain."

"Maybe," said the old groom, with a sidelong glance, "maybe it's because she's a thoroughbred. . . ."

Georgie coloured as she grasped what he meant.

"I must go in," she said hastily.

After prayers that morning, Miss Primrose said that she had an announcement to make.

"You all know what happened on the afternoon of Easter Monday," she said, in her direct way, "and I want to tell you that I have discussed the matter with the staff, and we are all agreed that the event should be commemorated in some way. Every year, therefore, the twenty-eight of March shall be a school holiday. Naturally it will not very often coincide with Easter Monday, but it will be on the day of the annual Lennet fair. We must decide later on how we shall celebrate it. Hands up those who like the idea."

Twenty-nine hands shot into the air. The thirtieth, still bandaged, did not move, as its blushing owner was wondering what to do. But it was seized—quite gently—by Susan, and waved amongst the rest.

"Good," said Miss Primrose, smiling at the staff. "This is our first tradition, made in our first term. I think that

118

all of us who are present now will remember it as long as we live. Perhaps in after years, when we are all scattered, we shall think of the Grange on this day, and write to one another or come back to spend a few hours at the school. Yes, Teepoo?" she asked, as the black hand went up again.

"I like to say, I remember, Miss Primrose. I celebrate every year, back in own country. I, and my people, and the children of my children's children!" said Teepoo, with great earnestness.

She meant that even in far-away Africa, future generations would remember a certain Easter Monday at the Grange school. Georgie was not the only one to feel moved by that promise.

"And now," said Miss Primrose, "time's getting on, and you must go to your form-rooms. But before you go, can anyone suggest a good name for our day? Please offer suggestions as quickly as you can."

They all stood there, frowning and racking their brains. They were trying to think of something descriptive and impressive, and at the same time pithy. The juniors and middle school looked hopefully at the prefects, obviously expecting one of them to rise to the occasion. But the prefects were gazing hopefully at the staff.

It was Susan who suddenly exclaimed "Donkey Day!"—and, absurd and unsuitable as it was, Donkey Day it remained through the years.

CHAPTER TWELVE

TWO weeks later, the term came to an end. There were no examinations this time, but there was an end-of-term party, followed by the inevitable orgy of packing and exchanging addresses. And then came the very last day.

Ruth and Anne needed Pierrot in the holidays, so he and the Thurstons' horses were loaded into a transport-van, and waved off the premises by all the girls. The rest of the horses were remaining at the Grange, in Maxwell's charge.

Penelope was staying too. Georgie went to say good-bye to her on the last morning, and kissed her brown velvet muzzle.

"I wish I could take you home," she said, "but you'll be happy here, and you love helping to mow the lawns. But when I leave school, you shall come and live with us always, even if we've got real horses by then."

Penelope seemed to wink, and then, throwing back her head, she indulged in the loudest bray that any of the girls had ever heard. Barbara pulled a face and covered her ears, as she was standing somewhere near, but her grin was not unkind, and everyone else looked with affection at the little donkey.

"Girls, didn't you hear the breakfast-bell?" cried Matron, who had bustled out to collect them all. "Please come in at once—time is short, and the girls who are leaving by train must be ready in half an hour."

Georgie, Susan, Teepoo, and the three Thurstons were among these, so they obediently rushed indoors, but were so excited that they could not eat much breakfast. Their luggage had gone down to Lennet Magna the night before, so when they had said good-bye to Miss Primrose, and waved a last farewell to the horses, they bundled into the school car and Maxwell drove them down to the station. Miss Briac was in charge, and in festive mood like the rest.

They all travelled together as far as Fontayne Junction, and then Georgie remained in the carriage alone, while the others caught the London train. She hung out of the window, vigorously waving a hand which, though still bandaged, was no longer painful. She thought fleetingly of Erasmus and the old lady with the apples. How long it seemed since she, an apprehensive new girl, had shivered on this platform!

And then her train started again, and she was really on the way home. What holidays these would be! First of all, her father would be coming home any day now, and after she had had two weeks of fun alone with the family, Susan and Patience were coming to stay, and Teepoo would pay her brief visit to Wychwood. The weather was lovely, so there would be picnics and tramps on the moors, and Peter, she knew from his letters, would be able to join in them now.

Georgie sat and hugged herself, mastering an impulse to get out and push the train. . . .

And now—here was Driscoe station! She rushed to the window, knowing that her mother would be on the platform. Yes, there she was, and Peter was with her, tall and upright, having discarded both glasses and stick. And behind him was another figure—her father, who must have landed earlier than they had expected.

"Daddy!" Georgie shrieked, and all but plunged to destruction.

Mr. Kane looked bronzed and well as he greeted his over-joyed daughter. Several minutes passed before anyone was able to utter a coherent remark.

"And now we must get home as quickly as we can," Mrs. Kane said at last. "I promised Gerry and the twins. If it hadn't been for your luggage, the whole family could have come to meet you."

"Oh, how I'm longing to see everyone and everything!" cried Georgie. "How is my angel Toby?"

"Very remote," said Peter. "There's been a vast spring cleaning, and he took a poor view of it. He hasn't purred for a week."

Wychwood at last! And there were the twins and Gerry, waiting impatiently at the gate. And behind them, wearing a terrible paper hat saved from a Christmas cracker, was Uncle Archie!

Georgie was actually glad to see him

To her own surprise, Georgie was actually glad to see him. She leapt out of the car and rushed at her brothers, knocking her head against Rough's so that they both saw stars, and shaking Gerry's correctly-outstretched hand. Then Uncle Archie gave her a suffocating embrace, and his hat fell off.

"Well, well, Curly-locks in person!" he boomed. "Or Diana, as we'll have to call her now. Diana the Huntress —eh! Welcome home, my dear! I thought you'd ride all the way back, or wasn't Penelope up to it? Ha ha!"

"Penelope's a darling, Uncle Archie, and I do thank you for her—Oh, there's Aunt Milly! And—*why*," cried Georgie, catching sight of a smiling face framed in white hair, looking out of the dining-room window, "I do believe the Great-Grandies are here!"

She raced into the house, and found that this was indeed the case.

"This is another celebration, dear child," said her great-grandmother, kissing her, "to make up for the one you couldn't attend. How well you look! Marcia, there's no doubt that the Grange, with all its excitements, must be a healthy place."

Mrs. Duncan stood laughing in the doorway.

"Well, Miss Georgie—well, I don't know! Such goings on. And looking twice the girl you used to be, I do declare! I tried to catch King Toby, to tie a ribbon round his neck, but he went off in a huff—and I can hear the turkey frizzling in the oven, so—" Mrs. Duncan, overcome by excitement, fled to the kitchen.

"Why, here's a letter waiting for me!" said Georgie, pouncing upon a white envelope. "It's from Teepoo." She tore it open. "Oh, *listen!*" she gasped:

Spot is yours now. I give him to you. No time for riding. My father, your father, Miss Primrose, all know. This is my secret. Pony of your own.

TEEPOO.

"Spot?" said Gerry. "What a name for a horse! You'll have to change it when she's left the school."

Georgie shook her head, her eyes like stars.

"I'll never change it. Just think of it—a pony of my very own!"

"Lunch will be ready in about ten minutes," said Mrs. Kane.

Georgie took the hint, and rose from the floor where
123

she had been playing with Velvet and Plush, now quite big dogs. She ran upstairs to wash her face and brush her hair, and Gerry followed, though her plaits were, as usual, beyond reproach.

"I say, Georgie," she began, rather awkwardly, "I didn't mean to be nasty—I think the Grange must be a thrilling sort of school, and it'll be fun when Susan and Patience and Teepoo come to stay. And," she finished nobly, "Spot is quite a good name. . . ."

"Oh, Gerry!" Georgie smiled at her, comb in hand, "He's the loveliest pony—though he hasn't a spot anywhere. I'll teach you to ride him one day."

Just as they were taking their places round the beautifully-decorated table, a round golden face appeared at one of the windows. A pair of agate eyes glowed like headlamps, and the handsomest whiskers in Dockleford twitched as King Toby recognized his mistress. She flew to let him in, and he wound his tail in a loving death-grip round her neck.

"You may let him sit on your knee just this once," said Mrs. Kane, forestalling Georgie's request. "But it's not to become a habit. It's just because this is an extra special day."

"It's an extra special lunch, too. Golly!" breathed Tough, as the turkey appeared, with bread sauce and everything—just like Christmas. Rough clasped his hands in ecstasy.

"I wish you two weren't going to be away when Sue comes," Georgie laughed: "you'd have a lot in common! Though perhaps in one way it *is* just as well. . . ."

"Ah, Curly-locks, I don't suppose you've had a square meal since you left home?" said Uncle Archie, who would believe to the end of his life that people were starved at school.

"Well, not like this," Georgie answered, with a patience she would not have shown three months ago. "Think what a lot of turkeys we should need! But we do have lots to eat."

"What is this strange noise I hear?" asked Great-grand-father, looking round.

"It must be the boiler," Mrs. Kane said distractedly, and then laughed. "No, it's King Toby, singing a pæan because Georgie's back."

Yes, he had found his purr again. He sat with folded paws on the wanderer's lap, expressing his joy in the only way he knew.

"I wish I could do that," said Georgie, as Mrs. Duncan came in with the Christmas pudding. "I'm purring inside, anyway!"

"Later you must tell us all about it, my dear," said her great-grandmother. "It seems a most interesting school—and quite different from Laurel Villa."

"One thing is certain," Peter said to Georgie, under cover of the general conversation: "that hat-band *was* a lucky omen. It was 'G for Georgia' after all."

"It nearly wasn't, though," she told him seriously. "I was a frightful cuckoo to start with. It wasn't easy at first. Nearly everyone was nice enough but I couldn't fit in. I mean, I wouldn't."

Peter nodded. "I know. I guessed by what you *didn't* say in your letters. I'm glad you didn't worry Mother by telling her how things were."

He did not add that their mother too had guessed.

Fruit and nuts succeeded the pudding.

"Speech, speech!" cried Uncle Archie, who was longing to make one himself.

"Yes, come on—speech!" roared the twins, dragging their sister to her feet.

Poor Georgie turned scarlet, and looked round at all the happy, expectant faces. Her parents were smiling at her, well pleased by what they saw. The Great-Grandies, too, were waiting eagerly to hear what she had to say. Her brothers and Gerry were beating some sort of tattoo on the table, Uncle Archie was busily filling up the glasses with lemonade, and Aunt Milly was actually getting out her little lace handkerchief, in case the speech should prove too affecting! Mrs. Duncan was hovering in the doorway, arms akimbo, thinking of the story she would have to tell Lily later on.

"Say something—anything," coaxed Peter.

"All right," said Georgie, striking a bargain: "I will if you will. You first!"

So, to save her embarrassment, he stood up and improvised a parody of a poem they both knew well.

"Sweet Stay-at-home has wandered far—
She knows now what adventures are!
We hope she'll keep the heart that's kind,
But much we're glad she's left behind!"

Everyone applauded, being in a mood to be amused at anything. Peter bowed with simpering modesty, and sat down again.

"Now *your* turn!" said Uncle Archie, turning to Georgie with the air of a Lord High Executioner.

"I don't think I can make a speech," she laughed, as she hugged the still-purring Toby, "but I'd just like to say that I'm glad, too, that I've left certain things behind—if I have—like being scared of horses. Because now I've got a pony of my own, and—" she paused, then ended in a rush, "and I wouldn't have missed the first term at the Grange for anything in the world."

Good Riding
by Christine Pullein-Thompson
Illustrated by Christine Bousfield

Christine Pullein-Thompson, famous for her popular
pony novels, takes you step by step from your first
riding lesson to that thrilling first clear round.

With illustrations on every page, *Good Riding* covers
mounting, your hands, your seat, the aids, pace and
control, schooling, hacking, learning to jump, coping
with problems, tack—and more ambitious activities
like pony clubbing, hunting, show jumping, gymkhanas, etc.

Learn to ride well, from the very beginning, and discover
for yourself the excitement and fun to be found in that
very special partnership—a good rider on a well-schooled
pony.

Armada

Pony Care from A-Z

by Charlotte Popescu
Illustrated by Christine Bousfield

What is a hackamore? How much should you feed a pony? How should you treat a girth gall? How can you tell a horse's age?

The answers to these, and a thousand other questions, can be found in this fact-filled encyclopedia, together with all you need to know about grooming, feeding, ailments, tack, grazing and stabling.

An invaluable, pocket-sized handbook—easy to look up and with scores of clear illustrations. A mine of information and helpful hints for all pony-lovers.

Publication: July 1975

Armada